Praise for
SCHOOL DAYS

"The best Spenser novel since *Early Autumn*."
—The Associated Press

"Plenty of entertainment . . . The two-fisted P.I. is in good form and his creator in fine fettle here." —*Los Angeles Times*

"A colorful assortment of dubious characters."
—*Entertainment Weekly*

"Spenser fans . . . will be thrilled to have their wisecracking Boston private eye back again . . . navigating the perilous shoals of suburban discontent and ripped-from-the-headlines horror stories—with only his fanciful German pointer, Pearl, to keep him company." —*New York Post*

"Spenser returns! He fights, he flirts, he cooks, he wisecracks, he quotes poetry. This thirty-third outing for the Boston private eye is one of the most psychologically astute and well-choreographed entries in the entire series. This is a high point in one of the genre's classic series." —*Booklist* (starred review)

"A pleasure . . . another solid installment in this fine, enduring series." —*Publishers Weekly*

"Vintage Parker . . . Everyone interested in mystery and contemporary writing in general should read at least one of the Spenser novels." —*Library Journal*

"Robert B. Parker is at the top of his game . . . *School Days* [is] one of the best and most timely books Mr. Parker has ever written." —*Midwest Book Review*

"A crackling yarn." —*Boston Magazine*

continued . . .

THE SPENSER NOVELS . . .

> "ONE OF THE GREAT SERIES IN THE HISTORY OF THE AMERICAN DETECTIVE STORY."
> —*The New York Times*

COLD SERVICE

When his closest ally is attacked, Spenser redefines friendship in the name of vengeance. "One hot mystery."
> —*The Washington Post*

BAD BUSINESS

A suspicious wife and a cheating husband pose a few dangerous surprises for Spenser . . . "A kinky whodunit . . . snappy . . . sexy."
> —*Entertainment Weekly*

BACK STORY

Spenser teams with Jesse Stone to solve a murder three decades old—and still cold as death. "Good and scary. This [is] superior Parker."
> —*The Boston Globe*

WIDOW'S WALK

Spenser must defend an accused murderess who's so young, rich, and beautiful, she *has* to be guilty. "Delicious fun. Bottom line: A merry *Widow*."
> —*People*

POTSHOT

Small-town Arizona is the home of big-time crime—and a psycho known as The Preacher. "Outrageously entertaining."
> —*The New York Times Book Review*

SCHOOL DAYS

Robert B. Parker

BERKLEY BOOKS, NEW YORK

THE BERKLEY PUBLISHING GROUP
Published by the Penguin Group
Penguin Group (USA) Inc.
375 Hudson Street, New York, New York 10014, USA
Penguin Group (Canada), 90 Eglinton Avenue East, Suite 700, Toronto, Ontario M4P 2Y3, Canada
(a division of Pearson Penguin Canada Inc.)
Penguin Books Ltd., 80 Strand, London WC2R 0RL, England
Penguin Group (Ireland), 25 St. Stephen's Green, Dublin 2, Ireland (a division of Penguin Books Ltd.)
Penguin Group (Australia), 250 Camberwell Road, Camberwell, Victoria 3124, Australia
(a division of Pearson Australia Group Pty. Ltd.)
Penguin Books India Pvt. Ltd., 11 Community Centre, Panchsheel Park, New Delhi—110 017, India
Penguin Group (NZ), Cnr. Airborne and Rosedale Roads, Albany, Auckland 1310, New Zealand
(a division of Pearson New Zealand Ltd.)
Penguin Books (South Africa) (Pty.) Ltd., 24 Sturdee Avenue, Rosebank, Johannesburg 2196,
South Africa

Penguin Books Ltd., Registered Offices: 80 Strand, London WC2R 0RL, England

This is a work of fiction. Names, characters, places, and incidents either are the product of the author's imagination or are used fictitiously, and any resemblance to actual persons, living or dead, business establishments, events, or locales is entirely coincidental.

SCHOOL DAYS

A Berkley Book / published by arrangement with the author

PRINTING HISTORY
G. P. Putnam's Sons hardcover edition / September 2005
Berkley international edition / July 2006

ISBN: 0-425-21091-X

BERKLEY®
Berkley Books are published by The Berkley Publishing Group,
a division of Penguin Group (USA) Inc.,
375 Hudson Street, New York, New York 10014.
BERKLEY is a registered trademark of Penguin Group (USA) Inc.
The "B" design is a trademark belonging to Penguin Group (USA) Inc.

PRINTED IN THE UNITED STATES OF AMERICA

10 9 8 7 6 5 4 3 2 1

FOR JOAN: *hasn't it been one hell of a ride to Dover.*

SUSAN WAS AT a shrink conference in Durham, North Carolina, giving a paper on psychotherapy, so I had Pearl. She was sleeping comfortably on the couch in my office, which had been put there largely for that purpose, when a good-looking elderly woman came in carrying a large album of some kind and disturbed her. Pearl jumped off the couch, stood next to me, dropped her head, and growled sotto voce. The woman looked at her.

"What kind of dog is that?" she said.

"A German shorthaired pointer," I said.

"Aren't they brown and white?"

"Not always," I said.

"What's her name?"

"Pearl."

"Hello, Pearl," the woman said, and walked to my client chair and sat down. Pearl left my side, went and sniffed carefully at the woman's knees. The woman patted Pearl's head a couple of times. Pearl wagged her tail slightly and went back to the couch. The woman put her large album on my desk.

"I have kept this scrapbook," the woman said to me, "since the day my grandson was arrested."

"Hobbies are nice," I said.

"It is far more than a hobby, young man," the woman said. "It is the complete record of everything that has happened."

"That might prove useful," I said.

"I should hope so," the woman said.

She placed it on my desk. "I wish you to study it."

I nodded.

"Will you leave it with me?" I said.

"It is yours," she said. "I have another copy for myself."

The woman's name was Lily Ellsworth. She was erect, firm, white-haired, and stylish. Too old for me, at the moment, but I hoped Susan would look as good as Mrs. Ellsworth when we got to that age. Being as rich would also be pleasant.

"And after I've studied it, ma'am," I said, "what would you like me to do."

"Demonstrate that my grandson is innocent of the charges against him."

"What if he's not?" I said.

"He is innocent," she said. "I will entertain no other possibility."

"What I know of the case, he was charged along with another boy," I said.

"I have no preconceptions about the other boy," Mrs.

Ellsworth said. "His guilt or innocence is of no consequence to me. But Jared is innocent."

"How'd you happen to come to me?" I said.

"Our family has been represented for years by Cone, Oakes," Mrs. Ellsworth said. "I asked our personal attorney to get me a recommendation. He consulted with their criminal defense group, and you were recommended."

"Do they represent your grandson?" I said.

"No. His parents have insisted on hiring an attorney of their own."

"Too bad," I said. "Cone, Oakes has the best defense lawyer in the state."

"If you take this case and need to consult him," Mrs. Ellsworth said, "you may list his fee as an expense."

"Her," I said.

Mrs. Ellsworth nodded gravely and didn't comment.

"Do you know who they have hired?" I said.

"His name is Richard Leeland. He is my son-in-law's fraternity brother."

"Oh," I said.

"You don't know of him," Mrs. Ellsworth said.

"No, but that doesn't mean he isn't good."

"Perhaps not," Mrs. Ellsworth said. "But being Ron's fraternity mate is not in itself much of a recommendation."

"Ron being your son-in-law," I said.

"Ron Clark," she said. "I still remember, approximately, a passage in *The Naked and the Dead* where someone describes a man as 'Westchester County, Cornell, a DKE, and a perfect asshole.' Mailer could have been writing of my son-in-law. Except that Ron grew up in Greenwich and went to Yale."

"A man can overcome his beginnings," I said.

"I wonder if you have," she said. "You seem a bit sporty to me."

"Sporty?" I said.

"A wisenheimer."

"Wow," I said. "It's been years since someone called me a wisenheimer."

"I may not be current in my slang," Mrs. Ellsworth said. "But I know people. You are a wisenheimer."

"Yes," I said, "I am."

"But not just a wisenheimer," she said.

"No," I said. "I have other virtues."

"What are they?" she said.

"I am persistent, and fearless, and reasonably smart."

"And modest," Mrs. Ellsworth said.

"That too," I said.

"If I hire you for this, will you put Jared's interests above all else?"

"No," I said. "I put Susan Silverman's interests above all else."

"Your inamorata?"

"Uh-huh."

"That's as it should be," Mrs. Ellsworth said. "Any other problems I should be alert to?"

"I don't take direction well," I said.

"No," she said. "I don't, either."

"And," I said, "you have to understand that if your grandson is guilty, I won't prove him innocent."

"He is not guilty," Mrs. Ellsworth said.

"Okay," I said. "I'll do what I can."

2

I STOOD AT my window on the second floor and watched
Mrs. Ellsworth as she came out of my building and
rounded the corner, walking like a young woman. Pearl got
off the couch and came over and looked out the window
with me. She liked to do that. Mrs. Ellsworth got into a
chauffeur-driven Bentley at the corner of Berkeley and
Boylston.

"She can afford me," I said to Pearl.

Late summer was in full force in the Back Bay. But, Au-
gust or not, it was gray and showery, and quite cool, though
not actually cold. Most of the young businesswomen were
coatless under their umbrellas. I watched as the Bentley,
gleaming wetly, pulled away from the curb and turned right

onto Boylston. The driver would probably turn right again at Arlington, and then go up St. James Ave. to the Pike and on to the western suburbs, with his wipers on an interval setting. I watched for a bit longer as two young women in bright summer dresses, pressed together under a big golf umbrella, crossed Boylston Street toward Louie's. Summer dresses are good.

When they had crossed, I turned back to my desk and sat down and picked up Mrs. Ellsworth's scrapbook. Neatly taped on the cover, an engraved calling card read 'Lily Ellsworth,' with an address in Dowling. I opened the scrapbook and began to read. Pearl went back to the couch. She liked to do that, too.

Two seventeen-year-old boys wearing ski masks had walked into the Dowling School, a private academy they both attended, and opened fire, each with a pair of nine-millimeter handguns. Five students, an assistant dean, and a Spanish teacher were killed. Six more students and two other teachers were wounded before the Dowling cops arrived, and the kids had barricaded themselves in the school library with hostages. The Dowling Police kept them there until a State Police hostage negotiator arrived with a State Police SWAT team standing by. Negotiations took six hours, but at three in the afternoon, one of the boys took off his ski mask and swaggered out, hands in the air, smirking at the cameras. The other one had disappeared.

The captured boy was named Wendell Grant. After two days of questioning, he finally gave up his buddy, Jared Clark. Clark denied his participation but had no alibi for the time, and was known to hang with Grant. After a few days in jail, Clark confessed. There was much more. Newspaper stories, transcripts of television and radio newscasts. Copies of police reports and forensic data; pictures of the boys. Neither was unusual-looking. Profiles of victims, interviews with survivors, and bereaved relatives. It didn't offer me much that was useful at the moment, though it would be a good source for names and dates later. And I didn't expect it to be a good source of facts, now or later.

When I got through reading the scrapbook, I called Rita Fiore.

"What do you know about a defense attorney named Richard Leeland?" I said.

"Never heard of him," Rita said.

"He's counsel for one of the kids who shot up the school in Dowling," I said.

"That kid shouldn't have a defense counsel I never heard of," Rita said. "But, I gather, at least he has you."

"His grandmother took your recommendation."

"Ah," Rita said. "That's who was asking. Everyone was so fucking discreet, I didn't know who the client was. How come they didn't hire me to help you or, actually, hire you to help me after they hired me?"

"Leeland was the kid's father's frat brother at Yale."

"Oh, God," Rita said.

"I know," I said. "Can you find out if he's any good?"

"Sure. I'll call the DA's office out there. What's in it for me."

"Dinner?" I said.

"At my house?"

"Sure. You get a date, I'll bring Susan, it'll be swell."

"You smarmy bastard," Rita said.

"You can't get a date?" I said.

"I had other plans," Rita said.

"I thought you were seeing that police chief from the North Shore," I said.

"I was," Rita said. "But he loves his ex-wife. You. Him. Every winner I find is in love with somebody else."

"Maybe that's not an accident," I said.

"Fuck you, Sigmund," Rita said.

"Or not," I said. "Susan's in North Carolina. I'll buy you dinner at Excelsior."

"How easily I settle," Rita said. "I'll meet you there at seven."

"Have your secretary make us a reservation," I said.

"My secretary?"

"I don't have one," I said.

3

DOWLING IS WEST of Boston. High-priced country
with a village store and a green, and a lot of big shade trees
that arch over the streets. As I drove along the main street, I
passed a young girl with long blond hair and breeches and
high boots, riding a bay mare along the side of the street,
and eating an ice cream cone. It might have been pistachio.
I pulled into the little lot in front of the village store and
parked beside an unmarked State Police car and went in.
There was a counter and display case opposite the door, and
a few tables. In the back of the store were shelves, and
along two sides were glass-front freezers. Two women in
hats were at one table with coffee. A young couple who
looked like J. Crew models were having ice cream at another

table. Alone at a third table was a stubby little guy with thick hands and thick glasses, wearing a tan poplin suit and a light-blue tie. I took a wild stab.

"Sergeant DiBella?" I said.

He nodded. I sat down across from him at the table.

"Healy called me," he said. "I used to work for him."

There were a few crumbs on a paper plate in front of DiBella.

"Pie," I said.

"Strawberry rhubarb. Counter girl told me they make it themselves."

"I better have some," I said. "Don't want to offend them."

"Make it two," DiBella said.

The pie was all it should have been. DiBella ate his second piece just as if he hadn't eaten a first one. We both had coffee.

"I've read the press accounts," I said, "of the school shooting."

"They're always on the money," DiBella said.

"Sure," I said. "I just wanted to test you against them."

A couple of local girls came in wearing cropped T-shirts and low-slung shorts, showing a lot of postpubescent abdomen. We watched them buy some sort of iced coffee drinks.

"Be glad when that fad is over," DiBella said.

"I'll say."

"You got kids?" DiBella said.

"No."

"I got two daughters," he said.

"So you'll be really glad," I said.

The girls left.

"Healy says the Clark kid's grandmother hired you to get him off."

"I like to think of it as *establish his innocence*," I said.

DiBella shrugged.

"Grant fingered him," DiBella said. "He confessed. You got some heavy sledding."

"But nobody actually saw him in the school," I said.

"He was wearing the ski mask."

"So you only have Grant's word."

DiBella grinned. "And his," DiBella said. "'Course, he could be a lying sack of shit."

I nodded.

"Where'd they get the weapons?"

DiBella shook his head. "Don't know," he said.

"Not family weapons?"

"Nope, far as we can tell, neither family kept weapons."

"So two seventeen-year-old kids in the deepest dark center of exurbia come up with four nines," I said.

"And extra magazines," DiBella said.

"Loaded?" I said.

"Yep."

"All the same guns?"

"No," DiBella said. "A Browning, a Colt, two Glocks."

"Same ammo," I said. "Different magazines."

DiBella nodded.

"The magazines and the guns were color-coded with Magic Marker," he said.

"Sounds like a plan," I said.

"Yeah. The thing is, they planned how to do it pretty good. But they didn't seem to have any plan for afterwards."

"You mean to get away," I said.

DiBella nodded.

"They explain that?" I said.

DiBella smiled. "They don't explain shit," he said. "All they say is we done it, you don't need to know why."

"Or how the second kid got away with the cops around the building."

"My guess? He took off his mask and ditched his guns and ran out with the other kids early in the proceedings."

"Must have been a Chinese fire drill," I said.

"Especially before our guys showed up. When it was just the local cops."

"Did you get there?"

DiBella nodded.

"Me, everybody. I came in with the negotiation team. SWAT guys were already there. The bomb squad showed up a little after me. There were two or three local departments on the scene. Nobody in overall charge. One department didn't want to take orders from another department. None of them wanted to take orders from us. Took a while for the SWAT commander to get control of the thing. And when he did, we still didn't know who was in there, or how many. We didn't know if the place was rigged. We didn't know if they had hostages, or how many. We'd have shot somebody if we knew who to shoot. Kids were jumping out windows and running out fire doors."

"Who went in?"

"Hostage negotiator. Guy named Gabe Leonard. Everybody was milling around, trying to figure how to get in touch inside, and the bomb-squad guys were trying to figure how to tell if the place was rigged. I was trying to get a coherent story from anybody, a student or teacher who'd been inside and was now outside, and Gabe says, 'fuck this,' and puts on a vest and walks in the front door.'"

"And nothing blew up," I said.

"Nothing," DiBella said.

We were out of coffee. I got up and got us two more cups.

"Gabe walks through the place, which is empty, like he's walking on hummingbird eggs. There's nobody else in there except the bodies, and finally the kid, in the president's office, with the door locked. They establish contact through the locked door and Gabe eventually gets the kid to answer the phone. Kid says he will, and Gabe calls out to us and one of the hostage guys calls the number and patches Gabe in, and they're in business. Gabe, and the kid, and us listening in."

"How'd he get him out," I said.

"I'll get you a transcript, but basically, he said, 'Be a stand-up guy. Whatever you were trying to prove, you need to finish it off by walking out straight up, not have us come in and drag out your corpse.'"

"And the kid says, 'You're right,' and he opens the door and comes out," DiBella said. "Takes off his ski mask. Gabe takes his guns, and they walk out together. Gabe said he wouldn't cuff him, and he didn't."

"Until he got outside," I said.

"Oh, sure, then the SWAT guys swarmed him and off he went."

"Film at eleven," I said.

"A lot of it," DiBella said.

4

THE DOWLING SCHOOL was on the western end of town, among a lot of tall pine trees. I drove between the big brick pillars, under the wrought-iron arch, up the curving cobblestone drive, and parked in front, by a sign that said FACULTY ONLY. There was one other car in front, a late-model Buick sedan.

The place had the deserted quality that schools have when they're not in session. The main building had a stone façade with towers at either end and a crenellated roofline between them. The front door was appropriate to the neo-castle style, high and made of oak planking with big wrought-iron strap hinges and an impressive iron handle. It was locked. I located a doorbell and rang it. There was silence for a long time, until finally the door opened and a woman appeared.

"Hello," she said.

"My name is Spenser," I said. "I'm working on the shooting case and wondered if I might come in and look around."

"Are you a policeman?" the woman said.

"I'm a private detective," I said. "Jared Clark's grandmother hired me."

"May I see some identification?"

"Sure."

I showed her some. She read it carefully, and returned it.

"My name is Sue Biegler," she said. "I am the Dean of Students."

"How nice for you," I said.

"And the students," she said.

I smiled. One point for Dean Biegler.

"What is it you wish to see?" she said.

"I don't know," I said. "I just need to walk around, feel the place a little, see what everything looks like."

Dean Biegler stood in the doorway for a moment.

"Well," she said.

I waited.

"Well, I really don't have anyone to show you around," she said.

"That's a good thing," I said. "I like to walk around alone, take my time, see what it feels like. I won't steal any exam booklets."

She smiled.

"You sound positively impressionistic," she said.

"Impressively so," I said.

She smiled again and sighed.

"Come in," she said. "Help yourself. If you need something, my office is here down this corridor."

"Thank you."

Inside, it smelled like a school. It was air-conditioned and clean, but the smell of school was adamant. I never knew what the smell was. Youth? Chalk dust? Industrial cleaner? Boredom?

I had seen enough diagrams of the school and the action in the newspapers to know my way around. There were four offices, including Dean Biegler's, opening off the central lobby. The rest of the school occupied two floors in each of two wings that ran left and right out of the lobby. The school gym was behind the rest of the school, connected by a narrow corridor, and beyond the gym were the athletic fields. There was a cafeteria in the basement of the school, along with restrooms and the custodial facilities. A library was at the far end of the left wing. Stairs went to the second floor in stairwells on each side of the lobby. On the second floor above the lobby were the teachers' lounge and the guidance offices. I began to stroll.

They had come in the front door, apparently, and past the offices in the lobby and turned left down the long corridor that ended at the library. Each was wearing a ski mask. Each was carrying two guns. Each had a backpack with extra ammunition in magazines, color-coded to the guns they had. They shot the first teacher they encountered, a young woman named Ruth Cort who had no class that period, and who had probably been on her way from the teachers' lounge upstairs to the library. She had bullets from two different guns in her. But there was no way to say if she had been shot by one shooter with two guns, or two shooters, one gun each. In fact, they had never been able to establish who shot whom. The guns and the backpacks were simply left on a table in the library when Grant came out, and no one could identify which had been used by whom. The cops had tried backtracking, establishing who had what color coding on which gun, but the eyewitnesses gave all possible versions, and it proved fruitless. There was powder residue on two coveralls that the shooters had discarded in the library, but none on their hands, because they wore gloves. The gloves, too, were discarded, and there was no way to establish which pair belonged to whom. Both had powder residue on them.

The Norman Keep conceit ended in the lobby. The cinderblock corridor was painted two tones of green and lined with lockers, punctuated by gray metal classroom doors. I went into the first classroom. The walls were plasterboard painted like the corridor. There was a chalkboard, windows, chairs with writing arms. A teacher's table up front with a lectern on it. Chalk in the tray at the bottom of the chalkboard. A big, round electric clock on the wall above the door. It had the personality of a holding pen.

I could taste the stiflement, the limitation, the deadly boredom, the elephantine plod of the clock as it ground through the day. I could remember looking through windows like these at the world of the living outside the school. People actually going about freely. I tried to remember what Henry Adams had written. 'A teacher is a man employed to tell lies to little boys'? Something like that. I wondered if anyone had lied to little girls in those days.

I moved on down the corridor, following the route of the shooters. I was wearing loafers with leather heels. I could hear my own footsteps ringing in the hard, empty space. The shooters hadn't made it to the second floor. The first Dowling cops had shown up about the time the shooters reached the library, and the shooters holed up there. Hostages were facedown on the floor, including the school librarian, a woman of fifty-seven, and a male math teacher who had been in there reading the *New York Times*. I could almost feel their moment, complete control, everybody doing what they were told, even the teachers. The room was unusual in no way. Reading tables, books, newspapers in a rack, the librarian's desk up front. Quiet Please. I looked at some of the books: *Ivanhoe*, *Outline of History*, *Shakespeare: Collected Works*, *The Red Badge of Courage*, *Walden*, *The Catcher in the Rye*, *Native Son*. Nothing dangerous. No bad swearing.

The windows faced west. And the late sun, low enough now to shine nearly straight through the windows, made the languid dust motes glisten with its gaze. I walked to the back of the library, near the big globe that stood in the far corner. I would have stood there, where I could see the door and the windows, holding a loaded gun in either hand, in command. King of the scene.

The library door opened as I stood looking at the room, and two Dowling cops walked in. They were young. One was bigger. They were both wearing straw Smokey the Bear hats. Summer-issue.

"What exactly are you doing here?" the bigger one said.

"Reliving school days," I said.

"Excuse me?"

"School days," I said. "You know. Dear old golden-rule days."

They both frowned.

"Chief wants us to bring you over to the station," the bigger one said.

The fact that the chief wanted me didn't mean I had to go. But I thought it would be in my best interest to cooperate with the local cops, at least until it wasn't.

"I've got my car," I said. "I'll follow you down."

5

THE DOWLING POLICE STATION looked like a rambling, white-shingled Cape. The Dowling police chief looked like a Methodist minister I had known once in Laramie, when I was a little kid. He was tall and thin with a gray crew cut and a close-cropped gray moustache. His glasses were rimless. He wore a white shirt with short sleeves and epaulets and some sort of crest pinned to each epaulet. The shirt was pressed with military creases. His chief's badge was large and gold. His black gun belt was off, folded neatly and lying on the side table near his desk. His gun was in the holster, a big-caliber pearl-handled revolver.

"I'm Cromwell," he said. "Chief of Police."

"Spenser," I said.

"I know your name," Cromwell said. "Sit down."

I sat.

"Real tragedy," Cromwell said, "what happened over at that school."

I nodded.

"We got there as soon as we heard, contained it, waited for backup and cooperated in the apprehension of the perpetrators," Cromwell said.

I nodded.

"You ever been a police officer, Spenser?"

"Yes."

"Then you know how it goes. You do the job, and the press looks for some way to make you look bad."

I waited.

"We got some bad press. It came from people who do not know anything at all about policework. But it has stung my department, and, to be honest with you, it has stung me."

I nodded.

"We played it by the book," Cromwell said. "Straight down the line. By the book. And, by God, we kept a tragedy from turning into a holocaust."

"Should I be taking notes?" I said.

Cromwell leaned back in his chair and looked at me hard. He pointed a finger at me, and jabbed it in my direction a couple of times.

"Now that was a wiseassed remark," Cromwell said. "And you might as well know it right up front. We have zero tolerance for wiseasses around here."

I liked the *we*. I wondered if it was the royal *we*, as in *we* are not amused. On the other hand, it still seemed in my best interest to get along with the local cops. I looked contrite.

"I'll try to do better," I said.

"Be a good idea," Cromwell said. "Now what we don't need is somebody coming along and poking around and riling everybody up again."

I was back to nodding again. Cromwell liked nodding.

"So, who hired you?" Cromwell said.

I thought about that for a moment. On the one hand, there was no special reason not to tell him. Healy knew. Di-Bella already knew. On the other hand, it didn't do my career any good to spill my client's name to every cop who asked. Besides, he was annoying me. I shook my head.

"You're not a lawyer," Cromwell said. "You have no privilege."

"When I'm employed by an attorney on behalf of a client, there is some extension of privilege," I said.

"Who's the lawyer?" Cromwell said.

"I'm not employed by a lawyer," I said.

"Than what the hell are you talking about?" Cromwell said.

"I rarely know," I said.

I smiled my winning smile.

"What's our policy on wiseasses around here?" Cromwell said.

"Zero tolerance," I said. "Except for me."

Cromwell didn't say anything for a time. He folded his arms across his narrow chest and looked at me with his dead-eyed cop look. I waited.

Finally, he said, "Let me make this as clear and as simple as I can. We don't want you around here, nosing into a case that is already closed."

I nodded.

"And we are prepared to make it very unpleasant for you if you persist."

I nodded.

"You have anything to say to that?" Cromwell said.

"How about, Great Caesar's Ghost!" I said.

Cromwell kept the dead-eyed stare on me.

"Or maybe just an audible swallow," I said.

Cromwell kept the stare.

"A little pallor?" I said.

Cromwell stared at me some more.

"Get the hell out of here," Cromwell said finally.

I stood.

"You must have screwed this up pretty bad," I said.

"If you're smart, you son of a bitch," Cromwell said, "you won't be back."

"I never claimed smart," I said, and walked out the door.

At least he didn't shoot me.

6

FRESH FROM MY TRIUMPH with the Chief of Police, I thought I might as well go and charm the kid's lawyer, too.

Richard Leeland had an office in a small shopping center, upstairs over the village grocery. From his window you could look at the eighteenth-century meetinghouse which lent New England authenticity to the town common, so you wouldn't get confused and think you were in Chicago.

"Wow," he said, "a private eye. We don't run into many private eyes out here."

"Your loss," I said.

"I'm sure," Leeland said. "May I ask you a question?"

He was a tall, slim man with a well-tanned bald head. He looked like he'd be good at tennis or bike riding.

"Sure."

"Who hired you to try and clear Jared?"

"You don't know?" I said.

Leeland smiled.

"It's why I'm asking," he said.

I thought about it for a minute. It made no sense that he didn't know, and it made no sense for me to keep secrets from my client's lawyer.

"His grandmother," I said.

"Oh, God," Leeland said. "Lily."

"Oh, God?" I said.

"She means well," Leeland said. "but she's beginning to show her age."

I nodded. Leeland was silent, his left hand at his mouth, looking at me, squeezing his lower lip between his thumb and forefinger. I waited.

After a while he said, "Jared confessed, you know."

I nodded.

"The Grant kid says Jared was with him."

I nodded.

"Doesn't that seem like you really have no case?" Leeland said.

"I have a case," I said. "I just don't know the outcome."

"The boy's guilty," Leeland said.

"Mrs. Ellsworth thinks otherwise."

"For God's sake, Spenser. She wouldn't believe it if she saw him do it."

"So you're going to plead him?"

"Guilty, see if we can bargain."

"How about insanity?" I said.

"He knew what he did was wrong," Leeland said.

"Irresistible compulsion?" I said.

He shrugged.

"Won't fly," he said.

"You have a shrink talk to him?" I said.

"We have the Dowling Academy consulting psychologist."

I nodded. "Name?"

"Why do you want to know?" Leeland said.

"I want to talk with him or her."

"I don't know if I should tell you," Leeland said.

"You think I can't find the name of the Dowling Academy consulting shrink?" I said.

Leeland shrugged.

"Her," he said. "Dr. Blair, Beth Ann Blair."

"See," I said, "how easy that was?"

"Mr. Spenser," Leeland said. "The boy is guilty. I know it, his parents know it, everyone knows it."

"Except Mrs. Ellsworth," I said.

Leeland ignored me.

"My job," he said, "quite frankly, is to try and soften the consequences the best way I can."

I nodded.

"Have you ever tried a murder case?" I said.

"Not really."

"Not really? How do you not really try a murder case?"

"I guess I meant no, I haven't," Leeland said.

"Do you know who's prosecuting?"

"Bethel County District Attorney's office."

"Know the prosecutor?" I said.

"His name is Francis Cleary."

"Be interesting to know how many murder cases their guy has tried."

"I'm a damned good lawyer," Leeland said. "I resent what you're implying."

I nodded. Spreading goodwill wherever I went.

"No offense," I said. "Did you get him a deal for copping?"

"Excuse me?"

"Did he get anything from the prosecution for confessing."

"He confessed without coercion or enticement," Leeland said, "to the Chief of Police."

"Cromwell," I said.

"Yes. You've met him."

I nodded.

"Fine law officer."

I nodded.

"How about the other kid," I said, "Grant. He get any kind of deal for fingering Clark?"

"I don't represent him," Leeland said.

"Who does?"

"Firm in Boston—Batson and Doyle."

"Who's the attorney?" I said.

"Alex Taglio."

"You and he talked?"

"We have," Leeland said. "We don't entirely agree."

"What's his plan?"

"I'm afraid that's confidential among attorneys."

"Sure," I said. "How's the kid doing?"

"He seems very withdrawn," Leeland said.

"I can see why he might," I said. "I'll need to talk with him."

"He really doesn't have much to say," Leeland said.

"Maybe he will," I said, "if he talks to someone who can at least entertain the possibility that he's innocent."

"I'd prefer not," Leeland said.

"You won't set up a meeting?"

"His parents have requested that he see only them and me," Leeland said.

"They think he's guilty, too," I said.

"They have taken him at his word," Leeland said.

"Trust is a wonderful thing," I said.

7

Rita and I browsed the food stands that lined both walls in Quincy Market in midafternoon, selected our lunches, and I paid for them. We took our food to the rotunda and sat among the tourists and suburban teenagers to dine.

"We may be the only residents of this city in the building," I said.

"I know it's not hip," Rita said. "But I kind of like it here. It's very lively, and there's lots of stuff to see."

"Yeah," I said.

There were old people—almost certainly retired, they had the look—and white kids from Littleton and Plymouth wearing three-hundred-dollar sneakers and sloganed T-shirts and hats at odd angles, trying hard to look ghetto. There were harried-looking young men and women with strollers. There was a scattering of suits, mostly young, and noticeable numbers of solemn Asian tourists.

"There's not much to know," Rita said, "about Richard Leeland. Comes from money. Yale Law School. Joined his father's law firm. His father also comes from money. Nobody has to work very hard. Father's semiretired. Richard does the heavy lifting."

"Which is?" I said.

"Real estate closings, wills, that stuff," Rita said. "No criminal experience. You know who the prosecutor is?"

"Francis Cleary," I said.

"Oh, Jesus," Rita said. "He'll eat your guy alive."

"He's good?"

"Not only good but zealous. He started life as a Jesuit priest, then left and became a lawyer. He's the chief AD in Bethel County."

"Not driven by greed," I said.

Rita smiled. She had a slice of pizza, from the pointed end of which she took a small bite.

When she had chewed it and swallowed, she said, "He believes in good and evil."

"One of those," I said.

"One of those."

"He says there's no insanity defense."

"He got a shrink?"

"School psychologist."

"You talk to him?"

"No."

"Well, even if the shrink is good, and sometimes they're

not," Rita said, "oversimplified, an insanity defense is going to go something like this:

"<u>Expert:</u> Because of a flopp to the fanottim, the defendant suffers from irresistible compulsion.

"<u>Cleary:</u> How do you know he has a compulsion?

"<u>Expert:</u> I've interviewed him.

"<u>Cleary:</u> And he told you he had a compulsion.

"<u>Expert:</u> Yes.

"<u>Cleary:</u> How do you know it's irresistible?

"<u>Expert:</u> He acted on it. He couldn't help himself.

"<u>Cleary:</u> So if somebody commits a crime, and claims compulsion, the commission is proof that the compulsion was irresistible?

"<u>Expert:</u> Well . . ."

I held up my hand.

"Got it," I said.

"A good defense lawyer and a good expert, or maybe several, can shape this, make it work better than I've described," Rita said. "But there's no reason to think this guy is a good defense lawyer. If the kid is a credible witness on his own behalf, it would help."

"I haven't seen him yet, either."

"You sound like you're getting stonewalled," Rita said.

"Local police chief doesn't want me around. I figure that's because he botched the thing badly and doesn't want attention called."

"So why doesn't the kid's lawyer want you around?"

"Doesn't want me screwing up the kid's plea, if I had to guess."

"Which you do," Rita said. "Not having anything in the way of facts."

"He doesn't want me talking to the kid," I said.

"Bethel County Jail?"

"Yeah."

"I know people out there, you need any help."

"Healy can get me in there," I said.

"I'm sure he can," Rita said. "You talked to the parents yet?"

"Not yet."

"That might be interesting."

I nodded.

"Know a lawyer named Alex Taglio," I said, "works for Batson and Doyle?"

"Alex Taglio, yes. Used to be a prosecutor in Suffolk County before he decided to make money."

"Not unlike others," I said.

"I was a prosecutor in Norfolk County before I decided to make money. There's a huge difference."

"I can see that," I said. "He any good?"

"Yes. Alex is a good lawyer. Works hard. Who's he represent?"

"The other kid," I said, "Wendell Grant."

"He and Leeland get along?" Rita said.

"Leeland indicated no," I said.

"Perfect," Rita said. "They being tried separately?"

"I don't know," I said.

"Probably not. Same crime. What's Grant's defense?"

"Don't know yet," I said.

"What do you think of Grandma?"

"Smart," I said. "Tough."

"Not old and losing her grip?"

"No. Leeland sort of implied that, but I don't believe him. She seemed right there when I talked with her."

"Why would the parents want to discourage an attempt to find their son innocent of multiple murder charges?"

"Don't know," I said.

"You don't know shit," Rita said, "do you?"

"No," I said. "But it's okay, I'm used to it."

8

IT HAD BEEN a rainy summer, and it was raining again. It was a good late-summer rain, warm, no wind, but not so hard that it overcame your defenses. I wished I was walking in it, holding Susan's hand. Susan of course would rather face gunfire than walk in the rain and ruin her hair. But fantasy wouldn't be fantasy if it was simply factual. As we walked, I'd sing "Here's That Rainy Day" and sound great.

But Susan was in Durham, and Pearl refused to go out in the rain, whether I sang or not. So I sat at my desk in my office, with the overhead light making the gray day look grayer out my window, and made a list of people I still needed to talk with about Jared Clark. I had some sense that it would be wise to talk with Jared last. I hadn't taken the time to figure out why I felt that. But I saw nothing wrong with it. So I put his name last on my list. Of the others, the closest was Alex Taglio, the other kid's lawyer.

I put Pearl on her leash, and we went down the back stairs to the alley where I parked my car illegally. But I had drunk coffee with the meter maiden a couple of times and exposed her to my compelling smile, so she gave me a bye on the parking issue. At the door, Pearl spotted the rain and sat down suddenly.

"You're a hunting dog," I said to her. "Born for the rugged outdoor life."

She didn't move. I tugged gently. She continued to sit. I picked her up. She weighed seventy-five pounds, much of which was legs and feet. I had to sort of jimmy her through the door opening.

Batson and Doyle had offices on Washington Street, near Court Street. On the walk up, Pearl often stopped and sat and looked at me with disbelief. Sometimes she jumped up instead and tried to get under my raincoat. She was greatly relieved when we got to the building and into the elevator and up to the law offices of Batson and Doyle.

"Alex Taglio," I said. "He's expecting us."

"You are?"

"Spenser," I said.

The receptionist looked at Pearl.

"Poor thing," she said. "She's all wet."

"She doesn't mind it at all," I said. "She's a hunting dog."

The receptionist led us to a conference room and ushered us in.

"Mr. Taglio will be right with you," she said.

Pearl was ill at ease in strange places. She stayed close beside me while I took off my raincoat and hung it on a hat rack. She was sitting beside me with her ears a little flat when Taglio came in. She growled at him.

"Christ," he said. "How's she know I'm a lawyer?"

"Hunting dog," I said. "Keen nose."

Taglio nodded and went around and sat across the conference table from me and Pearl.

"She a pointer?"

"Yeah. German shorthair."

"Aren't they usually more white than she is?"

"Yep."

"What's she hunt?" Taglio said.

"Couches mostly," I said. "Sometimes a gum wrapper."

"You want to talk about Wendell Grant," he said.

"Yes."

"You're working for the Clark kid."

"Actually, I'm working for his grandmother," I said.

"She thinks he's innocent?"

"I don't know," I said. "She might not care. She wants to beat the charge."

"Good for her," Taglio said.

He was a little guy with a large nose and a lot of dark hair. His eyes were dark and close to each other and very shrewd-looking. He was clean-shaven, and if he was going out for an evening, he would probably have to shave twice. Pearl had relaxed a little and was looking around the room. She spotted a couch against the wall behind us and left me and got on it. She turned around eight times and lay down with her chin on her paws.

"They going to be tried together?" I said.

"Unless I can get it severed, which I doubt. Judge thinks why waste time with two trials when you can slam-dunk them both with one."

"Why would you want to sever?" I said.

"We off the record here?"

"Sure."

"Clark's lawyer is a moron," Taglio said. "He can't do criminal defense."

"Anything else?" I said.

Taglio studied me for a moment. Behind him, the rain fell pleasant and straight past the tenth-floor window.

"Like what?" he said.

"Like he doesn't want to get the kid off?"

"Every lawyer owes the client the best defense he can have."

"And Leeland?" I said.

"His best won't be much," Taglio said.

"You have an opinion on how much he wants to get the kid off?"

"Nope."

"What do you think of irresistible impulse?"

"He going to plead that?"

"He says not. Says the shrink won't support it."

"So why you asking?"

"Might find another shrink," I said.

"Case doesn't look good to you, either," Taglio said.

"Not too," I said. "What about irresistible impulse?"

"Won't fly," Taglio said.

"It sometimes does," I said.

"Yeah, and he had an irresistible impulse to run and hide after he did it," Taglio said.

"Knew it was wrong, couldn't help doing it," I said.

Taglio grinned.

"I know who the trial judge will be," Taglio said. "The Honorable C. A. Murphy thinks Freud is a fraud misspelled."

"You're not going for insanity?" I said.

"No."

"What's your defense?" I said.

"I'm trying to get him a deal," Taglio said.

I nodded.

"How about Clark's expert witness."

"Beth Ann?"

"Uh-huh."

Taglio smiled.

"I'm gonna let you talk to her," he said.

"Any chance they didn't do it?" I said.

"They caught my guy red-handed," Taglio said.

"And mine?" I said.

"He confessed, for crissake," Taglio said. "And my guy says he's the accomplice."

"You're trying to make a deal," I said.

"Sure, and that was part of it. But that's all he'll say. Cleary wants where they got the guns? Anyone else involved? Why, for crissake, they did it."

"Cleary's the ADA on the case?"

"Yeah."

"And he wants *why*?"

"This happened out there in horse country," Taglio said.

"Or at least the back half," I said.

"You got that right. But these people think they live in fucking Eden out there. Things like this can't happen in Eden."

"Except for the damn snake," I said.

"Whatever," Taglio said. "They hate these kids for reminding them that it ain't quite Eden, you know? They want to lynch them."

"They segregated in jail?" I said.

"Of course," Taglio said. "They wouldn't last ten minutes in the yard. Hell, they wouldn't last a full day free in Dowling."

"Death threats?" I said.

"Sure."

"Serious?" I said.

"Maybe."

"How about the families?"

"They've had some threats," Taglio said. "Dowling cops are keeping an eye on them."

"That's reassuring," I said.

Taglio shrugged. Pearl resettled herself noisily on the couch. The rain came quietly down.

"You really going to try and get this kid off?"

"Not if he's guilty," I said.

"He's guilty."

"I don't know that yet."

"You don't?"

"Nope."

"Well, I give you credit for optimism," Taglio said.

"Glass always looks half full to me," I said.

Pearl saw me stand and scrambled off the couch. I attached her leash, which was not easy because she was jumping around with her eagerness to go. Just like human life. You want something so bad you make it hard to get.

"Besides," I said, "I like his grandmother."

9

BETH ANN BLAIR was hot. She had long, honey-colored hair and a wide mouth with a petulant lower lip, and big blue eyes. She was not in any way fat, but she was big and well proportioned, and sumptuous and re-silient. She almost trembled with energetic awareness of her body.

"I have a friend who's a shrink," I said, while I still had breath. "She's at Duke right now, giving a paper on the role of fantasy in romantic attachment."

"Really?" Beth Ann Blair said. "What is her name."

"Susan," I said. "Susan Silverman."

"I believe I know of her," Beth Ann said. "She's a Freudian?"

"I think she'd probably say she was eclectic."

Beth Ann Blair, Ed.D., had a small office with her name on the door in Channing Hospital, which was the regional medical center for most of Bethel County.

"I guess most of us are," she said. "You try everything and use whatever works."

"Talk to me about Jared Clark," I said.

"I prefer not to discuss my patients."

"You're going to have to discuss him in court," I said.

"Only up to a point," she said. "The law is quite specific on this."

"Are you ready to testify that he was in the grip of an irresistible compulsion when he shot those people? If he shot those people?"

"You question that he's guilty?"

"Just a working skepticism," I said.

"He has confessed, you know."

"Tell me what you can about him," I said.

"I saw him occasionally before the, ah, incident. I had office hours at the Dowling School several times a week. He came in a couple of times. He said he felt he was hurtling toward disaster and couldn't stop himself. He also said he felt as if a train were bearing down on him and he couldn't get off the tracks."

"Two different conditions," I said.

"Yes, in one he's propelled toward disaster; in the other it's propelled toward him."

Beth Ann was sitting sideways, facing me, at the end of her desk. Her skirt was short. She wasn't wearing stockings. Her bare legs were crossed. She seemed to stretch a little in her chair, the way a cat does, and uncrossed and re-crossed her legs. Susan always dressed down and wore understated makeup when she was working. She said the patient should not be distracted by her appearance. Beth Ann's appearance was distracting the hell out of me.

"Did you pursue that?" I said.

"He refused to come back. Said shrinks were all crazy anyway, and he wasn't."

"Have you talked with him since the event?" I said.

"After he was arrested, the police asked me to speak with him."

"And?"

"He said he did what he had to do and there was no turning back from it."

"And on that you're going to try for an irresistible compulsion plea?"

"We are hoping that he will talk with me more freely before we get to trial. If we went to trial today, I really couldn't argue the compulsion very well."

"Prosecution send in a shrink?"

"Yes. But Jared refused to speak with him."

Outside the window of Beth Ann's office, the rain still fell. It was colder rain today and was pushed a little more by the wind. Inside the office, it was bright and warm.

"Do you, in fact," I said, "regardless of what you can testify to, think Jared was in the grip of compulsion?"

"I don't know."

We sat for a time then. Beth Ann seemed comfortable enough with the silence. She rearranged her legs again. If she kept doing that, it was possible that I might begin to bugle like a stallion. Which would not be dignified. Beth Ann smiled at me and took a business card from her desk and wrote on the back.

"Perhaps you will want time to digest what we've discussed," she said. "I've written my home phone number on the back, should you need to reach me. Call anytime. I live in Lexington."

"Thank you," I said.

My voice sounded hoarse to me. I put the card in my shirt pocket and stood up.

"I'm sure we'll be in touch," I said.

My voice *was* hoarse.

"I do hope so," Beth Ann said.

10

HEALY GOT ME an interview with Jared Clark at the Bethel County Jail. DiBella took me over and walked me to the interview room.

The room was gray—walls, floor, and ceiling—with no windows. The gray door was metal and had a small window in it, covered with wire mesh, through which a guard could watch the proceedings. There was an oak table in the room, and four straight chairs. I sat at the table. DiBella waited outside.

Jared Clark looked badly out of place in his jail coveralls when two guards brought him in. He wasn't very big, and I was pretty sure he didn't shave yet.

One of the guards said, "You're with Sergeant DiBella."

I said I was.

The guards put Jared in a chair opposite me.

"Be outside," the guard said. "Bang on the door when you're through."

I said I would.

Jared sat back in his chair with his arms folded and looked at me scornfully. I took out one of my business cards and put it in front of him. He looked down and read it without touching it. Then he looked at me, and snickered faintly and shrugged. I folded my arms across my chest and leaned back in my chair and shrugged back at him. Neither of us spoke. The Bethel County Jail was a new facility. It was air-conditioned. I could hear the white sound of cool air moving through the vents. In the far background, I could hear the darker sounds of jail life.

We did this for a while.

Jared had light brown hair cut short. His nose was small and sharp. His mouth was thin and not very wide. He was short and seemed wiry. His hands were small. It was possible, of course, that Jared would outlast me. I knew he had no place special to go, and that staring it out with me was as pleasant as his day was going to get. On the other hand, he was seventeen and alone in a scary place, whereas I was not seventeen, and I was tougher than Bill O'Reilly. I might mean something to him. He'd need to know what.

And he did.

"So, what are you," he said finally.

"I've been hired to save your ass," I said.

He snickered again. We went back to quiet again.

"Who hired you to do that?" he said after a while.

"Your grandmother," I said.

He nodded.

"She thinks you're innocent," I said.

He nodded, and shrugged and smirked. I was tiring of the smirk.

"Care to tell me what happened that day in the school?" I said.

"Me'n Dell took out a lot of assholes," he said. "Needed taking out."

"Dell being Wendell Grant?"

"Sure."

"Can you name them?" I said.

"Who?"

"The people you took out."

For a moment, I thought he actually saw me. But it passed quickly.

He shrugged.

"How many did you take out?" I said.

He shrugged.

"Why did they need it?"

"They were assholes."

"And you could tell that how?" I said.

"Whole school was assholes," he said.

And smirked.

"Lot of that happening," I said.

He didn't say anything. I didn't say anything. We were back at it.

After a while he said, "How much she pay you?"

"Your grandmother?"

"Yeah. How much she paying?"

I told him.

"She can afford it," he said.

"Your lawyer wants to plead you crazy," I said.

Jared shrugged.

"You okay with that?" I said.

Shrug.

"You crazy?" I said.

"You ever kill anybody?" he said.

"Yes."

"You crazy?"

"No."

He smirked.

"Are you comfortable spending the rest of your life in the jug?" I said.

He shrugged.

"Have you thought about it? Sixty, seventy years?"

Shrug.

"Can't do the time," he said, "don't do the crime."

I was quiet for a moment.

"You don't think it'll happen," I said.

He shrugged.

"You don't think you're going away forever."

He shrugged again *and* smirked. What range.

"Even though you confessed," I said.

Shrug, smirk.

"You know something I don't know?" I said.

He snickered. And shrugged. And closed with a smirk. Three for three. I had really broken through.

We sat for a while longer.

I stood up.

"This has been great," I said.

He stayed seated, looking at the middle of my chest.

"Next time, you might want to extend your emotional range."

"Huh?"

"Work on sneering," I said.

I went and knocked on the door to get out. Behind me, I heard Jared snicker.

11

IT WAS DARK by the time Pearl and I got home. The rain had stopped, but the air was still heavy with its threat. The first thing I did when we got into my apartment was feed Pearl. It prevented her from crying and following me around, bumping my leg with her head. Then I made myself a tall scotch and soda and took it with me and stood in the front window and looked down at Marlboro Street. It was wet from the day's rain, and the streetlights made it gleam. Up the street, a white Explorer pulled up, and a well-dressed woman got out and headed into one of the town houses on the city side of the street. Even in the dim light, I admired her backside as she walked up the front steps. She rang the bell. I studied her backside. After a moment, someone opened the front door and a runtish Jack Russell terrier came out and barked at her, and then ran back in and she followed. The door closed. The white Explorer pulled away. I drank some scotch and looked at my watch. It was 8:35. Here and in North Carolina. We usually talked before she went to bed. I drank some more scotch. Pearl came and looked out the window with me for a moment and didn't see anything to engage her. She turned away and went into the living room and got up on the couch.

The excitement of the woman with the good-looking butt had passed. Marlboro Street was peaceful again. I thought about calling Susan. It was early. Eleven o'clock was the more-or-less scheduled time. She probably wouldn't be there. Probably out to dinner with someone other than me. If I called and she wasn't there, it would make me feel a little unhappy twinge in the pit of my stomach. Better to wait.

I drank some scotch.

I couldn't think of any way I could possibly keep them from sending Jared Clark away for the rest of his life. He said he did it. He showed no remorse. And it was certainly hard to like him. Besides, he deserved to do some time for aggravated smirking. I had deposited the retainer, but I hadn't spent it. I could give it back to Mrs. Ellsworth and tell her the kid was guilty as charged.

My glass was empty. I went to my kitchen and added fresh ice and Dewar's and a lot of soda.

"Kid's a creep," I said to Pearl.

She opened her eyes on the couch and looked at me without raising her head. I sat on the living-room side of my kitchen counter.

"I wonder if Mrs. Ellsworth knows that?"

Pearl seemed disinterested.

"She must have some idea," I said.

I drank some scotch.

"There's no one in there," I said to Pearl. "Unless it's all denial and bravado, and there's a scared little kid in there."

Pearl had no reaction.

"It doesn't feel like denial," I said. "It feels like empty."

I liked the way the tall glass looked with the pale scotch and soda over the slick ice, and the hint of moisture glossing the outside of the glass. I liked the way the ice felt against my upper lip when I drank.

"Malt does more than Milton can. . . ." I said.

Pearl had heard me say it before.

"Always thought Auden said that until some guy corrected me at one of Susan's parties. He said it was Housman. I was scornful of the poor, dumb, pretentious bastard, but I felt in fairness I should look it up."

Pearl's breathing was steady on the couch. I wasn't sure she was listening.

"It was Housman," I said.

I drank some scotch. My apartment was thick with silence. The scotch made it seem full of portent.

"I hate when I'm wrong," I said.

Pearl took no notice.

"I can't tell her," I said.

Pearl shifted and stuck her feet in the air and leaned them against the back of the couch and looked at me upside down for a moment before she closed her eyes again.

"I don't actually know he's not innocent," I said.

"Why would he lie?"

"Maybe he's crazy."

"Maybe he's simply bad."

"Bad?"

"You don't believe in bad, how you going to believe in good?"

"You metaphysical devil."

Pearl's position as she slept had caused her mouth to fall open and her tongue to loll out the left side of it. I looked at her.

"Yeah," I said. "That's about where I am."

12

IN THE MORNING it was still not raining, and still on the verge of it, when Pearl and I drove out to Dowling to visit Jared Clark's parents. They lived on some rolling green acreage, in a large, white house with a three-car garage.

It was cool with the foreboding rain. I left Pearl in the car with the windows partly open and walked to the front door and rang the bell. The woman who answered was only a few soft pounds short of heavy, with a kind of blank, blond prettiness that had probably gotten her cheerleading work in high school.

"Mrs. Clark?" I said.

"Yes."

"I'm Spenser."

"Oh, yes. Thank you. Please come in."

She was wearing a bright orange top and white pants and on her feet an attractive pair of flip-flops with orange straps to match her top, and in the center of each strap an ornamental plastic flower. I followed her into the enormous living room. It had the spontaneity of a furniture showroom, and gleamed with the spotless silence of for-company-only. Her husband was standing by the fireplace at the far end. He went perfectly with the room. He had on a pink polo shirt with a discreet alligator on the chest, pleated olive Dockers, and dark leather sandals. He was a nice-looking guy with sandy hair. His face had the same softness his wife's did. He walked to me and put out his hand.

"Ron Clark," he said.

We sat. I had the sense that my butt may have been the first one ever to press against the barrel-backed red armchair I was on.

I declined coffee, fearing I might spill some. Ron and his wife sat together across from me on a couch. They decided against coffee, too.

"How can we help," Ron said.

Here it was. I didn't like it, but at least it was quick. We didn't have to waste time talking about how rainy the summer had been.

"Do you believe he's guilty?" I said.

Mrs. Clark began to cry. Her husband put his hand on her thigh and patted it.

"He's our only child," Ron said.

I waited. Mrs. Clark continued to cry quietly, her head down, staring at her husband's hand on her thigh.

"Since he was born," she said quietly, "he had this distance about him."

The crying seemed to be tears only. Her voice was clear. Her husband nodded.

"It was like he was always thinking about something else," she said.

"Maybe if we'd had other children," her husband said. "Maybe if he'd had a brother . . ."

"He was never really a bad boy," his mother said. "His grades were good. He was never in trouble. He was just never with us, exactly."

We sat silently in the lifeless, perfect room.

After a while I said, "Do you believe that he's guilty?"

Still crying, without looking up, Mrs. Clark nodded yes. I looked at Ron Clark.

"My God," Clark said, "he confessed."

"Why do you suppose he did it?" I said.

Mrs. Clark's head was still down. She continued to cry quietly.

"We've asked each other a thousand times," she said.

"Sometimes," Clark said, "sometimes I think that maybe he did it for no reason. He did it because he wanted to."

"What does he say?" I asked.

"He doesn't," Clark said. "He won't talk about it."

"Is he mad at you?" I said.

"He doesn't seem to be," Clark said. "You think, Dot?"

"He doesn't seem to feel very much of anything," she said softly.

"His grandmother thinks he's innocent," I said.

"My mother-in-law," Clark said, "has a lot of money. It makes her think anything she wants to believe is right."

"Mrs. Clark?" I said.

"Often wrong but never uncertain, my father used to say."

"Was she close to Jared?"

"She thought so," Ron said.

"Did Jared like her?" I said.

"Hard to tell with Jared," Dot said.

"She wouldn't even know," Ron said. "She's so damned self-absorbed. She thinks he's innocent because he's her grandchild, and her grandchild can't be guilty of anything."

Dot Clark looked up at me. Crying had not helped her makeup any.

"Ron is quite hard on my mother," she said. "I know she cares for Jared."

"Were he and Wendell Grant close?" I said.

"I guess so," she said. "I didn't really know a lot about Jared's friends."

I looked at Ron. He shrugged.

"If he did do the shooting," I said, "do you know where he might have gotten the guns?"

They both shook their heads. It was a question every cop they'd talked to had asked.

"Do you wish me to prove him innocent?" I said.

They stared at me. Then at each other.

"We do not wish to have our hopes raised," Ron said carefully. "We are struggling to accept what is."

"Do you have any idea?" Dot said. "How could you possibly? We've lived here in this town for almost twenty years. We moved here to be part of this. To be part of a small town, and have friends, and know everybody and have everybody know us and . . ." She was looking straight at me and rolling her hands as she spoke, as if she were mixing bread dough.

"They all know us now," Ron said.

Dot finished her sentence as if he hadn't spoken.

". . . feel, like, the rhythm of community life. To belong to something."

"And now?" I said.

Ron shook his head slowly.

"How could you possibly prove him innocent?" Dot said.

"I don't know," I said. "May I look at his room?"

13

"MAY WE LEAVE YOU," Dot said. "We don't really like to come in here."

"Sure," I said. "I'll just sort of look around and think a little."

"Ronny and I will be downstairs," she said, and went.

I sat on the edge of the kid's bed. The room was blue and as soulless as the living room. The walls were darker blue, the ceiling a lighter shade. The bed was perfectly made with a brand-new blue quilt, with matching designer pillows stacked against the headboard. There was a bureau against the far wall, and a closet. A television sat on top of the bureau. There were no pictures on the walls. I opened the drawer in the bedside table. It was empty and clean. The drapes on the big window beside the bed were a darker blue than the walls. I looked under the bed. Nothing. Not even dust. I felt around under the mattress. Nothing. I stood and went to the closet. It was empty. I opened the bureau drawers. They were empty and lined with clean white paper. I went back and sat down on the kid's bed again.

As soon as he was gone they had cleaned out his room. It was as if they had emptied the room of him. Tried to render it pre-Jared, as if they could return life to the time when they had moved here and it was mostly possibility. There was no vestige of him. There had been no pictures in the living room. None of the cheap garish cardboard-framed school photographs that every parent had of every kid. No team photographs. No musical instruments. No CDs. It was as if he'd never existed, as if he'd never lain on this bed in the darkness and thought about sex or eternity or the American League. As if there had been no imaginary passions, no fantasized moments of derring-do, no terrifying moments of imagination when life's limitations nearly overwhelmed him. No graphic sexual conquests of women older than himself.

The room was empty and neutral and impenetrable. The only story it told me was that it had no story to tell. I got up and very carefully smoothed out the quilt where I had sat. I looked out the window. From here, I could see my parked car. I couldn't see clearly from here, but Pearl might have been sitting in the driver's seat. It was darker now than it had been, and rain began to spat disinterestedly against the window. I wondered if Jared had had a dog. I looked at the neat, color-coordinated, blank room upstairs in the neat, color-coordinated, blank house.

No. He didn't have a dog.

14

I WAS WALKING ACROSS the parking lot with Alex Taglio, toward the main entrance of the Bethel County Jail.

"What good does it do my guy to talk with you?" Taglio said.

"What harm?" I said.

"Say somehow, crazy as it is, you convince people that Clark isn't guilty," Taglio said. "My guy already rolled on him. Where would that leave us?"

"Maybe if he's innocent, he shouldn't be rolled on," I said.

"He is not innocent," Taglio said. "I said what if you *convince* people."

"If he's guilty, I don't want to get him off," I said.

"Oh, fuck," Taglio said, "I don't know what I'm arguing about. Rita already talked me into it."

"Sexual favors?" I said.

"I wish," Taglio said. "You ever?"

I shook my head.

"Married?"

"Sort of," I said.

"Sort of?"

"You?" I said.

"Mary Lou Monaghan," he said. "Five kids. She caught me fooling around, she'd cut off my wanker."

We went into the jail.

They got us seated, as far as I could tell, in the same interview room where I'd talked with Jared. When the guards brought Wendell in, they put him in the same chair. Might have been the same guards.

"First of all, Wendell," Taglio said, "Mr. Spenser's got no legal authority here. You don't have to talk with him if you don't want to."

"Like I got something else to do?" Wendell said.

He was a big, robust kid with pink cheeks and thick lips and smallish eyes. He had a white-blond crew cut. And he seemed to swagger even sitting down.

"He asks you something you don't like, you don't have to answer," Taglio says. "He asks you something and I tell you not to answer, you don't answer. Unnerstand."

"Sure, you bet, Alex. I do just what you say and everything'll be really fucking swell," the kid said.

Taglio sat back and let his face go neutral.

"I want to talk with you about Jared Clark," I said.

"No shit," Wendell said.

"Which one of you got the guns?" I said.

"Man, I told everybody already. I don't know where the guns came from. They were just there, man, when we decided we needed them."

"Why'd you need them?"

"To shoot up the fucking school, man. Whaddya think?"

"Whose idea was that?" I said.

"I told everybody this shit before," Wendell said. "Ten times. The cops, the lawyers, the jerkoff fucking shrinks. My old lady. Ten times. We wanted to do it. We did it. Here we are. End of story."

I nodded. Fun.

"What do you think of Jared?" I said.

"Huh?"

"Jared," I said. "What do you think of him."

"He bailed on me, man. He put his little sissy tail between his legs and snuck out, left me to deal with the cops."

"And it wasn't supposed to be that way?"

"Hell, no."

"How was it supposed to be?" I said.

"Stand-up, man. Two stand-up guys in there giving the cops the finger when they finally came in."

"But Jared got scared?"

"Looks like it," Wendell said.

"That why you rolled on him?" I said.

"Rolled?"

"You ratted him out to the cops."

"The fuck wasn't going to leave me with the bag."

"Plus, you got a deal," I said.

"That is between us and the District Attorney," Taglio said. "There's no reason for you to discuss that, Wendell."

"Whatever," Wendell said.

"So how do we know you didn't just make it up that Jared was there?" I said.

" 'Cause the fucker confessed, man. Would that be some kind of fucking clue."

"Good point," I said. "Must be a drag after being close with a guy all this time, he bails on you the minute things get rough."

Wendell shrugged.

"We wasn't so close."

"You enter into a plot to kill seven people with a guy you weren't close to."

"Sure, it was like, you know, business partners," Wendell said and laughed. "Wasn't like we was gonna get married or something."

"But you must have had reason to think you could trust him."

Wendell shrugged.

"But you couldn't," I said.

Wendell shrugged again.

"Make you mad?"

"Fuck him, man. I got it done without him."

"Got what done?" I said.

"I took care of business," he said.

"You shot those people without him?"

Taglio put a hand on Wendell's arm. Wendell looked at him. Taglio shook his head.

"I'm not talking about that," Wendell said.

"You know who shot whom?" I said.

Wendell shook his head.

"Did you shoot more or did Jared?"

Wendell shook his head.

"There were fifteen people shot," I said. "One of you must have shot more than the other unless both of you shot at least one of the same people."

Wendell shrugged.

"Maybe you both shot them all," I said.

"Fuck you," Wendell said. "I ain't talking to you no more."

"Everybody says that to me," I said. "Sooner or later."

15

WENDELL GRANT'S MOTHER'S name was Wilma. She ran a little health-food store near the center of town, with four tables outside, where you could sit and consume sassafras tea and bean sprouts on whole-grain bread. She was a pale woman with big, dark eyes and dark, straight, shoulder-length hair, which was beginning to show some gray. The day I went to see her, she was wearing an ankle-length gray dress with blue flowers, and leather sandals. There was no sign of makeup.

It was three o'clock in the afternoon. The store was empty of customers, and Wilma Grant sat with me at one of the small tables on the sidewalk outside the store. She drank some tea. I didn't.

"He just never . . ." she said.

I nodded.

"He never was what I wanted him to be," she said.

Her nails were square and clean, and devoid of polish. Her hands looked as if she washed them often.

"And Wendell's father?" I said.

She shook her head.

"No father?" I said.

"Except in a biological sense," she said. "I'm a single mother. His father is an anonymous sperm donor."

"And you've never been married?"

"No."

"Are you a lesbian?" I said.

"Not being married doesn't mean you are homosexual," she said.

"I know," I said.

"Are you married?"

"No."

She smiled slightly and nodded.

"I have had men in my life," she said. "But I never wished to marry them."

"But you wanted a family."

"I wanted," she said, "someone to share my life. I wanted to teach him and show him and talk with him and be with him. . . ." She stared down the long, still, tree-canopied, almost-empty street. "I wanted someone that belonged to me."

"Hard alone," I said.

"You have no idea," she said.

"Maybe I do."

"He was nothing like that. It almost seems as if from the

time he was born, he was angry and defiant and just exactly what I didn't want him to be."

"Tell me about him," I said.

She started to cry. I waited. After a while, she stopped.

"What was he like?" I said.

"He was a bully," she said. "My son, a bully. And he played football in school."

"Not a good thing?" I said.

"God, no. I think it's a brutal and dehumanizing game. All these loutish young men trying to hurt each other on the field, while the girls jump around and cheer and show their legs. It is frightful."

"What position did he play?" I said, just to be saying something.

"I don't know. I don't know anything about football."

"Did you ever see him play?"

"No."

"How was he academically."

She shook her head.

"He had no interest in the life of the mind," she said.

"Who taught him to shoot?" I said.

"Shoot?"

I nodded.

"I don't know," she said. "Certainly there have never been guns in my house."

"A woman living alone?" I said. "Not even for protection?"

"I would rather be killed," she said, "than take a life."

"No boyfriends, or uncles, or anyone that might have taught him?"

"No."

I nodded. We were quiet. A fat yellow cat came around the corner of the store and jumped up onto the table. Wilma picked him up and put him in her lap, where he curled into a fat yellow ball and went to sleep.

"Where might he have gotten the guns?"

"I don't know," Wilma said. "I know nothing of guns."

"Maybe the other kid got them," I said.

"Jared Clark?"

I nodded.

"I don't know. I barely know him."

"He was pals with your son, wasn't he?"

"I don't know."

"How did you come to get Alex Taglio for a lawyer?" I said.

"My father."

"Your father recommended him?"

"Yes."

"And your father's name is Grant?"

"Yes," she said. "Hollis Grant."

"He lives in town?"

"Yes."

"How's he know Taglio?"

"I don't know," Wilma said. "I suppose he asked one of his attorneys."

"He has attorneys?" I said.

"My father is a very successful man," she said. "Grant Development Corporation."

"In town?" I said.

"He lives here. His business is next town over."

"Is he close to his grandson?"

"Mr. Spenser, please don't put me through this anymore.

No one is close to Wendell. He carries my name. But he is so unlike me I tremble to think what a terrible person my donor must have been."

"You accept that he did it," I said.

"Yes. My father and I have employed Mr. Taglio to see that his rights are protected. But he has committed an unspeakable crime, and he should go to jail and stay there."

"So you don't wish him to get off?" I said.

"No. We can only try to help him spend his time in a less unpleasant prison."

"Like the easiest room in hell," I said.

She didn't say anything. She stroked the cat, and stared down the empty street, and shook her head a number of times.

16

"HOW MANY ROUNDS were fired in the school?" I said.

"Best count is thirty-seven."

"How many missed?"

"Seventeen," DiBella said.

"So some folks got shot more than once."

"One took four rounds," he said.

"Anything there?" I said.

"Nope, nothing we could find. Rounds came from two different guns, but whose and why four times? Don't know. One of them might have shot him twice with each of his two guns, or two of them maybe shot him twice each with one of their own guns."

"Who got the four hits?" I said.

"Ruth Cort, Spanish teacher."

We were in his car. Pearl, against all regulations, was in the back. She leaned her head into the front and sniffed DiBella's ear. He shook his head as if there were a fly in it.

"Anybody spots me with a hound in the car," he said, "I'll be running radar traps on the Mass Pike again."

"Claim it was my wife," I said, "and I'm insulted."

"Sure," DiBella said.

We were cruising through Dowling with the air-conditioning on low and the windows up. In the cool silence, the thick, rural greenery and the white, exurban houses outside the tinted glass of the car windows looked like some sort of theme-park display. New England Land.

"Know anything about Hollis Grant?" I said.

"Wendell's grandfather? Sure, everyone in this part of the state knows about him."

"Tell me what you know," I said.

"Big developer in central and western Mass," DiBella said. "Shopping malls. Civic centers. That kind of thing. He's not much into residential, I don't believe."

"Successful," I said.

"Yeah."

"Rich," I said.

"Yep."

"Connected."

"You bet," DiBella said. "Very active in politics. Donates a lot of money to a lot of people."

"He a gun guy?" I said.

"Hell," DiBella said, "I don't know."

DiBella pulled the car off the road and into an overlook area by a small river. The river dropped off some short falls and washed over some tumbled boulders, and made white water. The trees flourished near the river and stood high and thick above us. The moving water had a green tone to it. DiBella shifted in his seat a little and put his right arm over the back of the seat and patted Pearl.

"You think he's got something to do with this?"

"No idea," I said. "I'm just channel surfing. The guns bother me."

"Yeah," DiBella said. "Far as we can tell, there were no guns in either house, no shooters. Coming up with four nines is not all that easy for a couple of prep-school kids in Bethel County."

"And how to use them," I said. "We maybe forget, because we're used to guns. But you get a sixteen-, seventeen-year-old kid with no experience and no knowledge, give him a nine with an empty magazine and a box of bullets, and he's going to have trouble loading the bullets into the magazine, and putting the magazine into the piece, and getting a round up in the chamber."

"If he's mechanical and he has time, he could probably figure it out," DiBella said.

"Probably, but to hit twenty out of thirty-seven shots. . . ." I said. "In a real shootout, not on the range, with a handgun . . ."

DiBella nodded.

"I been shooting most of my life," he said. "I'd take that."

"There anyplace around here people shoot?"

"Local cops use our range in Talbot," DiBella said.

"Public welcome?"

"No."

"Any place where a private citizen could shoot?"

"Pretty good deer and pheasant around here in season," DiBella said. "I think there's a couple of hunting clubs got private range licenses."

"Names?"

"I can get them," DiBella said. "We haven't been chasing this as hard as you are."

"Of course not," I said. "You got one guy red-handed, and the other guy confessed. You got a slam dunk, why not take it?"

"It's not like they didn't do it," DiBella said. "We'll send them to jail."

"If they go," I said, "maybe somebody else needs to go with them."

"I got no problem with that," DiBella said.

"So where did they get the guns, and how did they learn to use them?"

"I thought you were supposed to clear this kid," DiBella said.

"I take what the defense gives me," I said. "I go where I can go, see what I find."

17

FROM THE WINDOW of Hollis Grant's unimpressive office in an industrial park he'd built, you could see straight
across the parking lot and observe the westbound lane of
the Mass Pike. Hollis himself was only a little better-
looking than his office. He was a strong-looking, over-
weight guy with not much hair and a lot of red face. He was
wearing khaki pants and work boots and a white dress shirt
with the sleeves rolled to his elbows. The office was small
and full of architectural drawings and spec books. There
was a drawing table along one wall. The walls were done in
plywood paneling. Hollis himself sat not at a desk but at an
old table littered with papers, a calculator, two phones, a
computer, and a big, clear-plastic T square.

"I'm looking into that shooting your grandson was involved in," I said.

"Why?"

"Make sure everything is as it seems to be."

"So what do you want with me," he said.

"Do you know Jared Clark?" I said.

"Kid that was with Wendell? No, I never met him."

"You close with your grandson?"

"Hard to be close with Wendell. There was no father in his life. I tried to provide him some of that. . . ." He shook his head. "But my daughter didn't want me to teach him any of the things I knew."

"Like what?" I said.

"Sports, business, tools, stuff that men might know."

"What did she want for him?"

He shook his head slowly.

"She wanted him to be her prepubescent toy forever."

"Difficult to achieve," I said.

"I tried to tell her he was going to grow up and would need to become a man. She said it didn't mean he had to be a man like me."

"What did she mean by that?" I said.

"You met her?" he said.

"I have."

"Miss Crunchy Granola. She was born in 1963 and grew up to be a hippie."

"Timing is everything," I said. "What's her problem with you?"

He shook his head again.

"I'm, oh, hell, I don't know. I'm too rough for her. I like

contact sports. I was in the Navy. I sometimes vote Republican."

"Good God!" I said.

"I know," he said. "I know."

"You must have had some success," I said. "He played football."

"Yes, God, she hated that."

"You teach him?"

"No, not really. The only thing I did, I got a box at Foxboro. I took him once to see the Pats play the Jets. She had a fit. I never took him again. Doesn't seem like such a fucking crime."

"You ever teach him to shoot?"

"Jesus, no," he said. "His mother would have . . . no. I never taught him to shoot."

"Somebody did. He and the Clark kid fired thirty-seven rounds and scored on twenty of them."

Grant didn't say anything.

"You shoot?" I said.

"I know how. I was in the service."

"Own a gun?"

"Revolver," he said. ".357 for plinking burglars."

"No semiautomatic weapons?"

"No. Revolver's so much simpler," he said. "And six rounds is enough."

"Why do you think he did what he did?"

Hollis sat for a time, looking at his fist resting on the tabletop.

"I don't know," he said. "I think Wilma blames me. I suppose I sort of blame Wilma."

He shook his head.

"Is there a Mrs. Grant?" I said.

"No."

"Was there?"

"Yes."

"And what happened to her?" I said.

"She left."

"When?"

"June twelfth, 1993."

"You know where she is?"

"No."

"Do you know if she's in touch with her grandson or her daughter?"

"No."

Spenser, grand inquisitor, give him a few minutes and he can find the topic to shut off any conversation. Maybe if I moved on.

"You said Wendell was hard to be close to. Why was that?"

"His mother filled his head with crap. I mean, she's my daughter, and I love her, but *her* head got filled with crap by *her* mother. Not the same crap, but she was fucked up, and she fucked up her kid."

"What did Wilma's mother fill her head with?"

"Ladylike," he said. "White gloves. Dinner parties. Her mother filled her head with silly shit, and Wilma rebelled."

"And filled her head with rebellious silly shit," I said.

"Yes."

"Have you seen Wendell since the shooting?"

"No."

"Because?"

"His mother has denied my access."

"Do you know Lily Ellsworth?" I said.

"Yes. Old money. Everyone knows Lily."

"She feels her grandson is innocent. She hired me to prove it."

"How you doing?" Grant said.

"So far," I said. "He looks guilty as sin."

"Like Wendell," Grant said.

"You know anything that would suggest he didn't do it?" I said.

"Except what I read in the papers," Grant said, "I don't know anything about the whole goddamned sorry mess."

"Sadly," I said, "me either."

18

SUSAN HAD BEEN SO compelling in Durham that one of the Duke professors had asked if she would stay into September and participate with him in his graduate seminar called Post-Freudian Therapy: the Practitioner's View. I missed her. I wasn't pleased. But I knew the recognition meant something to her, so I masked my displeasure.

"Oh, balls," I said on the phone.

"I knew you'd understand," Susan said. "And when I get home, we'll have a very nice time."

"Snivel," I said.

"That's my brave boy," she said.

We talked awhile about her meetings and my case. Her meetings appeared to be going better. At the end of her call, we talked dirty for a little while, which made me feel less fruitless. When we hung up, I went to the kitchen and made myself a drink and thought about supper. Pearl, in her wily canine way, divined my thoughts at once, and came and sat at my feet and looked at me closely. I gave her a dog biscuit.

"I got some cranberry beans," I said to Pearl. "And some local tomatoes and corn from Verrill Farm."

Pearl ate the dog biscuit.

"I'll start cooking that and see what develops," I said.

Pearl had finished her biscuit. Her gaze was again steady.

I shelled the beans from their long, red-and-cream pods and dropped them in boiling water and turned down the heat and let them simmer. I drank some scotch. I gave Pearl another cookie. Then I shucked the corn and put it into a pan with some cold water and brought it to a boil and shut off the heat and put the cover on the pot. Pearl had taken her cookie to the couch and eaten it. I took a small steak from the refrigerator and diced it into little pieces and cooked them rare in the frying pan. Then I turned them out onto a paper towel and let them sit.

Pearl returned.

"I can't keep giving you cookies," I said.

She looked at me steadily. I felt the steak dice. It was cool. I gave Pearl a piece. It must have struck her as exotic. She took it into the bedroom. My drink was gone. I took the corn from the pot with tongs and let it cool on the counter. Then I made a drink and took it to the couch and sat. Pearl came back from the bedroom and sat with me. I sipped my scotch.

"I'm missing something," I said to Pearl.

Pearl was a good listener, even if she didn't have much in the way of advice to offer. We sat quietly. I thought. I drank some scotch. Housman was right.

"First of all," I said to Pearl, "somebody said once that you probably can't figure out the truth, if you think you know ahead of time what the truth is supposed to be."

Pearl made a little sigh and settled.

"So I can't go at this trying to clear anybody. I just have to find out what happened and why."

Pearl's eyes were closed now. I got up and checked the corn and found it cool enough and cut the kernels off in long rows with a knife. I drained the beans into a colander, dumped them into a bowl with the corn, cut up some fresh tomatoes, added the steak, and tossed the whole deal with some olive oil, some cider vinegar, and salt and pepper. Then I let that sit for a while, freshened my drink, and came back to the couch. Pearl appeared to be asleep, but I pressed on.

"So what am I missing?" I said.

Pearl's breathing was even and soft.

"I'm asking the wrong people," I said. "Goddamn it, I'm talking to the adults."

I took a long, self-congratulatory pull on my drink.

Pearl made a soft sound. I bent toward her and listened more closely. She was snoring. I got up and put my supper on a plate.

"I should be talking to the kids," I said.

I drank my drink and ate my supper with some French bread.

19

IT WAS AFTER Labor Day and instruction was under way when I walked into the Dowling School. Sue Biegler brought me into the president's office, introduced me, and departed.

The president was a middle-sized man with thinning hair, so that close up, he was balder than you first realized. He wasn't fat, but he was soft-looking. His soft face had one of those perpetual blue shadows that no amount of shaving would eliminate. Nature is not fair. Too little hair, too much whisker. His name was Dr. Royce Garner.

"First," he said, "let me say that every one of us here at the Dowling School are heavy at heart about last spring's tragedy. And we stand ready to help you in any way we can."

"That's swell," I said.

"We do, of course, hope," he went on, "that we can put it behind us as quickly as we can, and get back to what we do best."

"Educating the young," I said.

"Exactly."

He leaned back a little, with his fingertips pressed together, delighted with himself.

"What is your doctorate in?" I said.

"Divinity," he said. "I am an ordained minister."

"How come you're a president," I said. "I thought prep schools had headmasters."

He smiled indulgently at my lay confusion.

"We are planning to expand into a junior college as soon as our fundraising for the venture is complete," he said. "It seemed appropriate to assume the title in our quest to give credibility to our capital campaign."

"Of course," I said.

He smiled again.

"So, how may I be of help?" he said.

"I'd like to hang around the school for a time," I said. "Talk with kids in their free periods, in the library, that sort of thing."

"Really?"

I nodded.

"What would you be chatting about?"

"Last spring's shooting," I said.

"We are trying to put that behind us, Mr. Spenser."

"Don't blame you, especially when you're trying to raise money."

"That is an issue, certainly," Garner said. "But it is the

well-being of the students that we are most concerned about. We cannot prepare them for college and a productive life with this terrible tragedy hanging ever over them."

"I understand," I said. "It is, however, an unresolved tragedy. I'm trying to resolve it."

"Unresolved?" Garner said. "How so?"

"We don't in fact know for certain what happened."

"We know that good people, many of them still children, were killed by two individuals who are in custody."

"We don't know why."

"And you think my students will know why?"

"Ever hopeful," I said.

President Garner wet his plump lips. He put his fingertips together in front of his chin.

"I'm afraid school policy will not permit it," he said. "I'm truly sorry."

"Who's in charge of school policy?" I said.

"Myself and, of course, the board."

"Of course," I said. "I bet that board is a collection of tigers."

He smiled.

"They are dedicated people," he said. "They care about the Dowling School."

"Isn't that ducky," I said.

"No need to be offensive."

"The hell there isn't," I said. "Everybody wants this to go away—you, the cops, even the parents of the alleged shooters."

"I believe they are more than alleged," Garner said.

"They are alleged until they are convicted," I said. "And that hasn't happened yet."

"That is something of an equivocation," Garner said.

"Normally, when everyone wants something to go away, it's because if it doesn't, it will cause them discomfort. Maybe you'll be revealed as a bad educator, or the cops will be revealed as bad lawmen, or the parents will be revealed as bad parents. And that will discomfort you all."

"I think that's about enough, Mr. Spenser."

"Almost," I said. "But I do want you to know that I am a carrier of discomfort. I am deeply committed to it, and I'm going to find out what happened."

"They killed people," Garner said. "Isn't that enough?"

"No," I said. "It's not."

"I'm ordering you to leave school property," Garner said. "If you return, I'll have you arrested."

I thought about saying "I shall return," decided it had been used before, and settled for walking out without a word and not closing the door.

20

IT TOOK ME a couple of days of hanging around outside the Dowling School, feeling like a pederast, to find where the kids congregated after class. It was a place called Coffee Nut, where they could sit in booths and drink coffee and eat doughnuts and smoke and impress one another. The owners of Coffee Nut had obviously written off the adult market they might have originally planned on, and decided to commit themselves to adolescence. There was music I didn't recognize playing loudly when I came in. The place was half full, and everyone turned to look at me, as if I had violated a segregation law. Except that I was, of course, poised and debonair. Otherwise, I might have felt ill at ease.

There were booths along one side and in the back. A counter ran along the other side. I sat at the counter next to a couple of schoolgirls who were giggling and whispering, maybe about me. *Oh, Spenser, you dashing rogue, you've still got it.* The girls were wearing what I would eventually discover most Dowling schoolgirls wore: short, pleated skirts and sleeveless tops. One was blonde with a pink top. One was brunette with a white top. I ordered coffee, which took a while, because I had to reject a half a dozen special coffee drinks, which I also didn't recognize. There were two high-school girls in tan uniforms working the counter and an older guy wearing a tan overseas cap that said COF-FEE NUT on it, who was making the coffee.

I turned and leaned my back against the counter.

"You girls go to Dowling School?" I said.

"Yeah," Pink Top said and giggled. "You?"

"Couldn't pass the entrance exam," I said. "Everybody in here from Dowling?"

"Sure," Pink Top said. "'Cept them."

She nodded at the people working the counter.

"You here last year when the shooting happened?"

"I guess so," the girl said.

They had thought it sort of fun to get into conversation with a large older man, especially because they were surrounded by friends. But now they were uncomfortable.

"My name's Spenser," I said.

White Top poked Pink Top with her elbow.

"See," she said. "I told you it was him."

Pink Top said, "We had an assembly about you."

"Hot dog," I said.

"Mr. Garner said we weren't supposed to talk with you."

"Why not?" I said.

"Mr. Garner said you were trying to ruin the Dowling School's reputation, and if you succeeded, we'd never get into a good college."

"Do you believe Mr. Garner?" I said.

They giggled again.

"Royce the Voice," White Top said. "The People's Choice."

"May I take that as a 'no, we don't believe him'?" I said.

"Royce is gross," Pink Top said.

"Or Groyce," White Top said, and they both giggled some more.

"What would happen," I said, "if he were right, and you didn't get into a good college?"

"My mother would kill herself," Pink Top said.

"My mother would call me a slut," White Top said.

"For not getting into a good school?" I said.

"She calls me a slut whenever she's mad," White Top said.

"You are a slut," Pink Top said.

"Takes one to know one," White Top said.

They both giggled some more.

"Did either of you know the guys involved."

"You know, casually. Say hi in the hall."

"Any thoughts on why they did what they did?"

The girls looked at each other for a moment. They were being asked to think.

"You know," White Top said, "what's amazing is it doesn't happen more often. You know? I mean, do you remember school?"

"I do," I said.

"Did you like school?"

"No."

"Good. It's all bullshit, you know. It's all the official pious crap."

"That's my memory of it," I said.

"So I don't know why they did it. But everyone's walking around, barely able to stand it, and"— she shrugged— "these guys went kaboom, I guess."

"Anything set them off?"

"I don't know," White Top said. "You, Janey."

"No clue," Pink Top said.

"Anyone in here knew them well?"

"Guys at that table played football with Dell," White Shirt said.

"Grant," I said.

"Yeah."

Pink Top swung her stool all the way around, which, given the shortness of her skirt, was pretty daring, and said, "Hey, Carly."

She was too young to interest me, but she got Carly's attention.

"This is the guy old man Garner warned us about."

"No shit," Carly said.

She was not too young for him. He admired her legs visibly as he walked over.

"This is Carly Simon," Pink Top said. "This here is . . . I forgot your name."

"Spenser," I said.

I took some cards from my top pocket and gave one to each of them.

"Name's Carl Simon," he said. "Everybody calls me Carly."

Carly was a prototype prep-school football player. He might even play small college ball, but would never go beyond that. He was short and muscular with a thick neck. He probably weighed 160 pounds.

"Carly's the football captain," Pink Top said.

"Running back?" I said.

"Yeah. Deep back out of a pro set. We went seven and two last year."

"And Wendell Grant was an offensive lineman," I said.

"Left tackle."

"Know him well?"

"On the field," Carly said.

"And off?"

"Off," Carly said, "he was a creepy fucker."

He said fucker sort of aggressively, to see if I would react. I maintained my composure.

"How so," I said.

"He hung with all townies," Carly said.

"Dowling's a day school, isn't it?" I said. "Aren't you all townies?"

"We're all from around here. But there's the kids go to Dowling. And the kids go to the Regional."

"Which is?" I said.

"High Meadow Regional," White Top said. "It's in Melwood."

"And you don't mix?" I said.

"Not much," Carly said.

"How about Jared Clark?" I said.

"Nobody knew him," Carly said. "That I know."

"He wasn't an asshole," Pink Top said. "He was just, like, not there, you know?"

"He didn't seem interested in anything the rest of us were interested in," White Top said.

"Anyone know him better?"

"Nobody I know," Carly said.

He looked at the two girls. They shook their heads.

"So where do the townies hang out?" I said.

"Place called the Rocks," Carly said. "Down back of the park, by the lake. They go over there, smoke some weed, drink beer."

"You ever been over there?" Pink Top said.

"Yeah, couple times. Bunch of assholes."

"Weren't you scared?"

"I go where I want to," Carly said.

"Did you witness the shootings?" I said.

All three shook their heads.

"We were on the second floor," White Top said, "Janey and me. They never got there."

"I was in American history," Carly said. "We jammed the teacher's chair under the door handle to the classroom and everybody got down. They never came in."

"Thanks for your help," I said.

"Pleasure," Pink Top said. "Dork Garner isn't going to tell me who I can talk to."

"Me either," White Top said.

"I'm glad he tried," I said. "Worked out well for me."

"Bet your ass," Carly said. "We were so ready to talk to you if we got the chance."

"Okay, let's really sock it to him," I said. "Ask around. Anybody knows anything, you have my card."

"You're an actual private eye," Pink Top said.

"I've begun to have doubts," I said.

"You must be," Pink Top said. "Says so right on the card."

"Oh, thank God," I said.

21

Two Dowling cops were leaning on a squad car outside the coffee shop. One of them stepped in front of me on the sidewalk.

"Chief wants to see you," he said.

"Everybody does," I said.

There was a black Chevy sedan with tinted windows parked on the curb behind the squad car. A cop in plainclothes got out of the front seat and opened the back door.

"In here," he said.

I looked into the backseat. Cromwell was there. I slid in beside him, and the plainclothes cop closed the back door and opened the driver's door to get in.

"Wait outside the car," Cromwell said.

The cop closed the door and went and leaned with the two uniforms on the squad car in front of us.

"This mean you like me?" I said.

Cromwell was wearing his big, terrifying pearl-handled revolver. I felt honored. Cromwell ignored my question. Probably felt it was frivolous. He looked at me with his eyes half closed. It was supposed to make my blood freeze.

"Optics are amazing, aren't they?" I said. "We can see out fine through the tint, but people outside can't really see us much."

"Shut up," Cromwell said.

The eyes behind the rimless glasses narrowed some more. I squinted back at him.

"Hard to see, isn't it," I said, "with your eyes three quarters shut."

"This is your last chance," Cromwell said finally.

"It is?"

"After this, it gets very rough."

"Oh," I said. "That's when."

The front windshield wasn't tinted. Through it, the three cops leaning on the squad car could look in at us.

"You might get hurt bad," Cromwell said, "resisting arrest."

"Gee," I said, "maybe this doesn't mean you like me."

"Do I make myself clear?" Cromwell said.

"Actually," I said, "I'm a little murky on some things. Like when your guys arrived, why did they secure the perimeter and stay there while the shooters inside kept shooting?"

"It was a hostage situation. Anybody knows anything about policework knows you don't go charging into a hostage situation."

"But it wasn't a hostage situation. It was serial murder in progress."

"We had no way to know that," Cromwell said.

"The sound of gunshots inside didn't suggest anything?" I said.

"Besides, it might have been booby-trapped."

"But it wasn't," I said.

"We had no way to know that, either."

"So you didn't go in."

"We weren't going in until we had proper intelligence and appropriate backup."

"You're telling me," I said, "you didn't go in because it might not be safe?"

"Goddamn it, that's not what I said."

"It is what you said; it's just not what you wanted me to hear."

Cromwell's voice had gotten hoarse as we talked.

"We contained it," he rasped. "Goddamn it, we contained it."

"You were scared," I said. "And you didn't know what to do. And there are some kids dead who would be walking around today if you'd gone in there sooner."

"You sonovabitch," Cromwell croaked.

He took his big pearl-handled gun out and started to point it at me. I took hold of the barrel before he leveled it and bent it back so the gun was pointing at the roof of the car. He struggled to level it. But I held it there. So we sat, sort of frozen in place. The three cops out front glancing through the windshield couldn't see much in the backseat, and whatever they saw didn't look like trouble. They stayed where they were.

"Let go," Cromwell said, "or I'll shoot."

"You're a small-town police department. You never saw anything like this before. You had no hands-on experience. You were scared. So you hunkered down and waited for the Staties."

"Let go," Cromwell said.

His voice was so thick, he seemed to be having trouble squeezing his words out.

"Okay, it was a fuck-up," I said. "And it cost lives. But it was sort of an understandable fuck-up, unless it was one of your kids got killed."

"Let go."

"It's the coverup that's going to kill you," I said.

Cromwell didn't speak. He had taken hold of his gun with both hands and was trying to force it down enough to point it at me. He couldn't. Then he tried to pry my fingers off the gun barrel. He couldn't.

Through the front windshield, I saw the three cops at the squad car turn their heads to stare at the coffee shop. I looked out the back in the same direction. The kids had come out of the coffee shop to see what was up. They stood in a ragged row on the sidewalk, watching.

I was holding his gun barrel with my left hand. I shifted slightly in the seat and, with my right hand, punched him in the crotch. He gasped and doubled over and I took the gun away. While he gasped against the pain, on the seat next to me, I snapped open the cylinder, took out the big .45 slugs, closed the cylinder, and put the empty gun back in his holster.

"You been hit in the balls before," I said. "You know the pain will pass. While it's passing, let me hold forth for a moment. I am going to find out what happened and why and where they got the guns, and how they learned to shoot, and then we'll see. I am going to share my concerns with the State Police Homicide Commander in Boston, guy named Healy. If he doesn't hear from me every day he'll be out here looking for me, and he'll know who to ask."

Beside me, Cromwell, still bent over, had started taking deep breaths.

"That aside," I said, "I got no reason to embarrass you. I will leave you out of anything I can, as much as I can, unless you're guilty as hell . . . or unless you annoy me."

Cromwell slowly straightened. His shoulders were still hunched, and he kept his hands over his groin, but he was sitting more or less upright.

"Where's my bullets," he said.

I handed the six big bullets to him. He took them and made no move to reload.

"I don't want trouble with you," I said.

He didn't look at me.

"But remember one thing," I said. "You don't want trouble with me, either. It might work out well if we gave each other a good leaving alone."

Cromwell still wouldn't look at me. I waited a moment. He didn't say anything. So I got out of the car. The three cops looked at me carefully. Several of the kids started to clap, and most of them joined in. I gave them a V-for-Victory sign. Cromwell never moved from the backseat.

Pink Top said, "You go, Big Daddy."

"I do," I said.

And did.

As I strolled off down the street toward my car, with the plaudits of the crowd still ringing in my ears, I had a sort of tense, targety feeling between my shoulder blades.

I'd had it before.

22

I HAD A DATE for a drink with Rita Fiore in the late afternoon at the Ritz Bar on Arlington Street. It was raining again, and the cars on Boylston Street had their headlights on early as I walked down from my office with my raincoat collar turned up and my Pittsburgh Pirates cap tugged down over my forehead. People were leaving work, and the sidewalk was a moving jumble of umbrellas. With my natural agility, however, I was able to avoid injury. Rita was at a window table when I got there.

"Why are you wearing a black hat with a P on it," she said.

"Pittsburgh Pirates," I said. "Goes with my raincoat."

Rita was drinking a martini. She had already ordered me

a scotch and soda, which sat waiting. I took off my hat and coat and put them on the floor and sat down in front of the scotch.

"Johnnie Walker Blue," Rita said.

"I deserve no less," I said and took a pull.

"Susan still gone?" Rita said.

"Yes."

"Is it possible she's not coming back?" Rita said.

"No."

"Well, it happened once before," Rita said.

"That was two other people," I said.

"So not this time?"

"No."

"Damn," Rita said. "Any chance we could pretend, like for an evening?"

"I could not love thee half so well," I said, "if I loved not honor more."

"Oh . . . fuck!" Rita said.

"Or not," I said.

"You probably didn't even quote it right."

"Everybody's a critic," I said.

She reached across and patted my hand.

"How's everything in Dowling?" she said.

"The community is united in its conviction that I'm a nosy pain in the ass and should be stonewalled."

"Poor baby," Rita said.

"The thing is, nobody, not even their parents, seems interested in how two teenaged boys acquired four semi-automatic handguns and ammo, and enough skill to hit two-thirds of their targets."

"Close range," Rita said.

"Maybe. But when people pick up a hammer for the first time, they miss the nail more often than that."

"So you're saying it wasn't the first time."

I nodded.

"Were these kids marginal?" Rita said.

"It's hard to tell," I said. "The Grant kid played football. The kids I've talked with so far say that Clark was sort of a nobody."

"Any pattern to who they killed?" Rita said.

The waiter came by. We ordered another round. He went away.

"I don't know enough yet," I said. "DiBella says no."

"He any good?" Rita said.

"Healy says he is."

"And Healy is good."

"Very," I said.

Trying to stay out of the rain, a youngish woman wearing a stylish red raincoat and walking a small dog pressed in against the window next to where I was sitting. I looked at her.

"Are you looking at her ass?" Rita said.

"I am," I said. "I'm a detective. It's my nature."

The waiter brought the fresh drinks.

"You are right across the table from one of the great asses on the East Coast, and you're looking at her ass out the window."

"I can't see yours," I said. "If you wanted to go outside and press it against the window . . ."

"In the rain?"

I shrugged. Rita grinned.

"Besides," she said. "I'm using it to sit on."

"What a waste," I said.

We each drank.

"Maybe they just hated school," Rita said.

I nodded.

"I was talking to some kids yesterday," I said. "One of them said something."

Rita waited quietly. For all her mouthiness, she had a great capacity for intelligent silence as needed.

"She said that everybody's walking around in school barely able to stand it, and these guys just went a little further and couldn't stand it. 'These guys went kaboom,' she said."

Rita nodded.

"My brother," she said, "married a nearly perfect knee-jerk upclass suburban mom. She's dreadful. But the poor bastard loves her, and there it is. When my nephew was three, she was worrying about getting him into the right preschool. Kid's fifteen now. He's under pressure to make sure he gets good grades so he can get into a good school. He needs to show good extracurricular activities to get into a good school. He needs to be popular with his classmates. Which means be just like them. Dress right, use the proper slang, listen to the proper music, go away on the proper vacations. Live in the right neighborhood, be sure his parents drive the right car, hang with the right group, have the right interests. He has homework. He has soccer practice and guitar lessons. The school decides what he has to learn, and when, and from whom. The school tells him which stair-well he can go up. It tells him how fast to move through the corridors, when he can talk, when he can't, when he can chew gum, when he can have lunch, what he is allowed to wear . . ."

Rita paused and took a drink.

"Boy," I said. "Ready for corporate life."

She nodded.

"And the rest of the world is telling him he's carefree," she said. "And all the time he's worried that the boys will think he's a sissy, and the school bully will beat him up, and the girls will think he's a geek."

"Hard times," I said.

"The hardest," she said. "And while he's going through puberty and struggling like hell to come to terms with the new person he's becoming, running through it all, like salt in a wound, is the self-satisfied adult smirk that keeps trivializing his angst."

"They do learn to read and write and do numbers," I said.

"They do. And they do that early. And after that, it's mostly bullshit. And nobody ever consults the kid about it."

"You spend time with this kid," I said.

"I do my Auntie Mame thing every few weeks. He takes the train in from his hideous suburb. We go to a museum, or shop, or walk around and look at the city. We have dinner. We talk. He spends the night, and I usually drive him back in the morning."

"What do you tell him?" I said.

"I tell him to hang on," Rita said.

She was leaning a little forward now, each hand resting palm-down on the table, her drink growing warm with neglect.

"I tell him that life in the hideous suburb is not all the life there is. I tell him it will get better in a few years. I tell him that he'll get out of that stultifying little claustrophobic coffin of a life, and the walls will fall away and he'll have room to move and choose, and if he's tough enough, to have a life of his own making."

As she spoke, she was slapping the tabletop softly with her right hand.

"If he doesn't explode first," she said.

"Your jury summations must be riveting," I said.

She laughed and sat back.

"I love that kid," she said. "I think about it a lot."

"He's lucky to have you. Lot of them have no one."

Rita nodded.

"Sometimes I want to take him and run," she said.

The wind shifted outside, and the rain began to rattle against the big picture window next to us. It collected and ran down, distorting reality and blurring the headlights and taillights and traffic lights and colorful umbrellas and bright raincoats into a kind of Parisian shimmer.

"I know," I said.

23

SINCE WE WERE WALKING through a park and down by the lake, away from any roads, I took Pearl off the leash and let her bound about like a rhebok. The rocks were an outcropping of basalt left by some vast meltdown some eons back. Scattered in the area were some boulders, probably deposited by a glacier some other eons back. The basalt sloped over the lip of a hill and down toward the lake shore. Scattered about on its surface were a bunch of prototype suburban dropouts who had been deposited more recently. I counted three girls and ten boys, plus one guy who was too big to be a boy. He was an obvious bodybuilder, heavily tattooed and of apparently mixed ethnicity. I guessed Asian and Hispanic.

Riding the smell of the lake was the rich scent of marijuana. Pearl smelled it and stopped. She was not bumptiously friendly. When she spotted the group, her ears went down and she came over beside me.

"My name is Spenser," I said. "I'm looking into the school shooting."

"Well yippee iyoh ki yay," one of the kids said.

He was a gangly guy with hair so red it was nearly maroon. He looked a little unfocused. Beside him, the big older guy stared at me silently. He had on jeans and motorcycle boots and no shirt. Most of his upper body was ornamented.

"I was wondering what you all could tell me about Wendell Grant," I said.

"So who's that with you," the red-haired kid said, "Dr. Watson?"

One of the three girls threw a pebble at Pearl. It missed, but Pearl shied a little closer to me. I looked at the girl. I knew how it was going to go, but there was no help for it.

"Next person bothers the dog, goes in the lake."

Everybody looked at the big guy with the tattoos. He remained seated on the rock.

"That's my girlfriend you talking to," he said.

"Good to know," I said. "Wendell Grant hang around with you all?"

"I'm talking to you, pal," the big guy said.

"Squint your eyes a little," I said.

He stood.

"What's that supposed to mean," the big guy said.

"Makes you look more dangerous," I said. "You squint up, like this, and you say, 'I'm talking to you, pal.' No emphasis on any of the words, you know. Scares the shit out of people."

"Jesus, mister, don't fuck with Animal," the red-headed kid said.

"Animal needs to be fucked with," I said, "about once a day."

Animal walked at me with his fists chest-high and tried to kick me in the groin. He was ferocious but slow. I turned away from the kick and hit him a straight left on the nose. The nose broke and began to bleed. I didn't want this to take long, because I didn't want Pearl to get scared and run off. I hit him with a flurry of lefts and rights while he was still trying to get over the initial pop on the schnozzle. He took a couple of steps backward, trying to cover up, trying to regroup. I put my hands on his shoulders and spun him and put my foot in the small of his back and shoved, and he stumbled and slid down the hill and fell in the lake.

I looked around. Pearl was about thirty feet away in a full, belly-scraping cower. I went over to her and squatted down beside her and put an arm around her.

"Okay," I said. "All over. Okay."

She sniffed at my mouth.

"Okay," I said.

She gave me a lap on the nose. I stood, keeping one hand on her neck, patting her. The silence around the Rocks was vast. I could still smell the weed, but I heard nothing. At the foot of the hill, Animal was sitting in the lake trying to splash water on his face. The blood from his nose was seeping pink through his hands.

"Jesus," the red-haired kid said.

"I'm looking for information," I said, "about Wendell Grant."

"I never seen anything like that."

I was still pumped, and it made me a little brusque.

"Care to see it again?" I said. "Throw something at the dog."

Nobody said anything. At the foot of the hill, Animal sat in the water. He wasn't splashing water on his nose anymore. He was simply sitting, slumped in the water, his reputation in ruins about him.

"Wendell close with anyone in the group."

Nobody spoke.

"Anybody got any idea why he might have shot up the school?"

Silence.

"Or where he got the guns?"

Silence. The three girls got up as if they were one. They were in full costume. A lot of hair. A lot of makeup. Cropped T-shirts that stopped well above the navel. Low-rider pants that barely covered the pubic bone.

"I'm sorry I threw something at your dog," one of them said. "I like dogs."

"You Animal's girlfriend?" I said.

"We all are," she said. "Can I pat your dog?"

"No."

They all three shrugged at almost the same time and moved away. Seeing the group diminish, the red-haired kid got to his feet.

"I gotta go, man," he said.

I took out a card and gave it to him.

"You think of anything, call me," I said. "You might as well get the reward as anyone."

"Reward?"

I nodded. He looked at my card and put it in the back pocket of his jeans and walked away. The rest of the kids left. At the bottom of the hill, Animal sat alone in the water. I stared down at him for a while, then I looked at Pearl, who was exploring where the kids had been sitting, in case they had left edible refuse. She was not successful, but there was no quit in her. She coursed back and forth among the rocks, exploring all possibilities. Hot on the trail of nothing much.

Like me.

After a while I said to no one in particular, "Okay."

Pearl looked up.

"Okay," I said again.

I jerked my head for her to follow and started down the hill.

24

I SAT AT THE water's edge on a small rock. Pearl moved along the edge of the lake, looking for frogs. Animal sat with his back to me, not moving, not saying anything.

"Three girlfriends," I said. "Way to go, Animal."

He didn't answer. His head was down, his hands resting lightly over his broken nose, sheltering it, not quite touching it.

"Put ice on it," I said. "I've had, I think, eight broken noses. They heal."

His head was forward on his chest. He didn't answer.

"You're going to be a tough guy, you need to be a lot quicker."

He didn't move.

"Or pick someone you can scare."

Nothing.

"They'll forget it," I said. "You can reestablish. Slap one of those asshole kids around and they'll think you're heroic again."

"I ain't forgetting it," he said in a thick voice.

"No, probably shouldn't. Make it a learning experience."

He stared at the pinkish lake water between his knees. His nose still dripped blood.

"I got connections," he said. "This ain't the end of it."

"You the candy man?" I said.

He didn't answer.

"Yeah, 'course you are," I said. "You're the one sells them dope."

He shook his head. It hurt. He stopped.

"You could probably get them a gun, too, they needed it," I said.

He was still.

"I'm not a cop," I said. "I'm only interested in Wendell Grant and the Clark kid."

He didn't speak.

"You sell them any guns?"

Silence. To my right, Pearl kicked up a frog from the growth at the water's edge, and it bounded ten feet out into the lake, with Pearl bounding right behind it.

"What's your name?" I said.

He didn't answer.

Pearl put her head underwater and pulled it out, but she'd missed the frog. She swam in circles, looking for it.

I said, "If I have to stand you up and take your wallet

and look at your ID, it'll start your nose bleeding again and probably hurt. What's your name."

"Yang," he said.

"First or last?"

"Last."

"What's your first name? "

"Luis."

"Luis Yang."

"Yes."

Pearl swam one more circle and gave up and came back into shore and began rummaging in the waterweeds again.

"Emergency room can clean that thing up and pack it for you. Maybe give you some pain pills."

Animal didn't move or speak or look at me. I stood up.

"Don't take aspirin," I said. "It'll make it bleed more."

Then I made a little chuck sound to Pearl, and she and I went back up the hill.

25

It was Saturday. Lee Farrell had come to spend the day with Pearl. This made Pearl happy because she liked Farrell, and he would almost certainly overfeed her.

So I was back in Dowling alone, sitting at a table on the sidewalk outside Coffee Nut in the bright morning with a large cup of coffee, cream, two sugars. The girl who had worn the pink top came by and saw me and sat down with me. Her top was white today. And her short pleated skirt was tan.

"Janey, isn't it?" I said.

"Yes."

"Can I buy you some coffee?"

"Black," she said.

I went in and got some and brought it back. She lit a cigarette.

"I heard you had a fight with Animal," she said.

I nodded.

"I heard you threw him in the lake," she said.

"He fell in the lake."

"They said you, like, creamed him," she said.

I smiled.

"I won the fight," I said.

She stared at me.

"Everyone is scared of Animal," she said. "The football players, everybody."

"He's pretty scary," I said.

"He's a perv," Janey said. "They're all pervs out there at the Rocks anyway."

I nodded. She kept looking at me.

"What's the perviest thing they do?" I said.

"All the girls have to, like, have sex with Animal," she said.

"Or what?"

"Or they can't hang out."

"Do they have any other boyfriends?" I said.

"If Animal says."

"How do you know so much about this?" I said.

"One of the girls went to junior high with me. I see her sometimes."

"What's her name?"

"It's really Annette George," Janey said. "But everybody calls her George."

"Was she there when I had the fight with Animal?" I said.

"Yuh." Janey giggled. "She threw the stone at your dog."

"You suppose we could talk with her?" I said.

"You and me?"

"Yeah."

"Sure, I guess so," Janey said. "I could call her."

"Why don't you," I said.

Janey took a cell phone out of her purse and dialed. I went to get us two more coffees. I bought us some doughnuts, too. Balanced nutrition.

"She'll meet us at the mall in an hour," Janey said.

"Melwood Mall?"

"Yes."

"Not here."

"God no."

"You don't want to be seen with her," I said.

Janey shrugged.

"Or she with you," I said.

Janey nodded.

"Or me," I said.

Janey nodded more vigorously.

"Of course," I said.

We drank some coffee.

"How come you could, like, beat up Animal so easy?" Janey said.

"Purity of heart," I said.

"Huh?"

"My strength is as the strength of ten, because my heart is pure?"

"What are you talking about?" Janey said.

"I rarely know."

"Seriously, how come? I mean Animal is . . ." She

spread her hands; words failed her in the face of Animal's prowess.

"It's what I do," I said.

"Beat people up?"

I shrugged.

"Like everything else," I said. "It helps to know how."

"And you know how?"

"I used to be a fighter," I said.

"You mean a boxer. Like whatsisname Lennox something?"

"Yeah. That kind," I said.

"Jesus," she said. "Is that why your nose is like that."

"Thanks for noticing," I said.

"Were you ever a champion or anything?"

"No," I said.

"But you're still, like, ah, good."

"You been a fighter," I said, "and you stay in shape, you don't lose that many fights outside the ring."

"You don't seem like a mean guy," Janey said.

"I don't?"

"No. You seem kind of nice."

"Damn," I said. "I'll have to work on that."

Janey nodded. Some kids drove by in a red Jeep Wrangler with the top down. They honked. She waved. She was with a celebrity. The guy who threw Animal Yang into the lake.

26

You could be in a mall in the food court and you could have no idea where in this great republic you might be. Same cuisine. Same décor. Same clientele. It was comforting. Anywhere in America, you could count on the same fried rice, the same cheese steaks, the same slice of pizza. We met George at a table near the souvlaki stand. She was enjoying a large Diet Coke and a cigarette. She didn't look at me when we sat down.

"Hi, Janey," she said.

Janey said, "Hi."

"Remember me?" I said.

George nodded. She had changed clothes, but the look

was the same. Cropped T-shirt, low pants. Her eyes were slathered with dark makeup, and her lips with dark gloss. She had silver rings on all her fingers. And her nails were painted black.

"Have you seen Animal?" I said.

She shook her head.

"Tell me a little about him," I said.

George looked at Janey.

"He's an okay guy," Janey said. "You know? You can, like, talk to him. He won't tell."

George nodded and looked back at me.

"Whatcha want to know?" she said.

"Animal get you dope?" I said.

"Yes."

"What?" I said.

"Mostly, like, weed," she said. "But whatever you want, you tell him, he gets it for you."

"Know where he gets it?"

"Some gang in Boston, I think," George said. "I think it's his brother's gang."

"Know the name of the gang?" I said.

"No."

"Wendell Grant hang with you guys?" I said.

"Some."

George stubbed out her cigarette and lit another one. She had a thin face. Under the makeup were dim traces of acne scarring.

"Dell do any dope?" I said.

"He was, like, heavy-duty," she said. "Coke, meth, lots of stuff."

"He get it from Animal?"

"Yeah, 'course. You get stuff around the Rocks, you get it from Animal."

"Dell tight with Animal."

"Nobody was tight with Animal. He is the Man, you know? I mean, everybody is scared of him and like, *sure Animal, anything you say, Animal.*"

"King of the Rocks," I said.

"Yes."

"Animal ever have a gun?" I said.

George looked at Janey again.

"I'm telling you," Janey said. "He's okay."

She was right, of course, but I wondered how she knew that. Probably didn't matter. I was now a celebrity and, more important, at this moment, I was her celebrity.

"Yeah, he had a gun. Him and Dell, like, used to shoot guns sometimes."

"What kind of guns?" I said.

"Little ones. You know . . . like . . . handguns!"

"Did you see what kind of handgun?"

"I don't know," she said. "Just, like, a gun you hold in your hand and go *bang bang.*"

"Square-looking or kind of round."

"Square, I guess."

"Shoot a lot of times without stopping?" I said.

"I guess."

"What did they shoot at?"

"Bottles, and boxes and stuff. Sometimes they'd find a stray cat and, like, shoot at it."

"Did Dell have a gun?"

George shook her head.

"Animal let him use one of his," she said.

"Animal have many guns?" I said.

"I don't know," George said. "I guess he could get them whenever he wanted them."

"From his brother?"

"I guess."

"Ever see Jared Clark around there?" I said.

"Jared? The phantom? No. He'd be too scared."

"You scared?"

"Yeah, of Animal."

"But you're his girlfriend."

"Sure. All the girls, you want to hang at the Rocks, you got to fuck Animal."

"What would happen if you didn't?" I said.

"Nobody, like, doesn't," she said. "You don't, you don't hang there."

"And you got to hang somewhere," I said.

"Acourse," she said.

27

"WHAT KIND OF DOG you say she was?" DiBella said.

"German shorthaired pointer," I said.

"And why has she got her head in my wastebasket?"

"Looking for clues," I said.

Pearl straightened from her exploration of DiBella's wastebasket with an empty yogurt carton in her mouth.

"See, now we know what you were eating," I said.

Pearl took the carton to the corner of the office and settled down with it.

"She gonna eat the fucking carton?" DiBella said.

"She'll probably chew it and spit it out," I said.

"On my fucking floor?"

"I'll pick it up," I said.

DiBella watched her for a moment, then looked at me and shook his head slowly.

"You know how many people come in here with a fucking dog?" he said.

"None?"

"That's right, none."

"They're obviously not fun like me," I said.

"And God bless them for it," DiBella said. "We got nothing on Luis Yang."

"How about his brother?"

"I talked with the gang squad in Boston."

"And?"

"They got nothing on Luis Yang, either," he said. "But there's a Jose Yang in a gang called Los Diablos."

"Clever name," I said.

"Yeah. Gangbangers are always imaginative. Usual stuff—deal dope, run a chop shop, fight other gangs."

"Guns?"

"Yeah. Gang squad says they have guns, probably got a connection. Probably could get more. Probably pretty much anything you wanted."

"So," I said. "Maybe we know where the guns came from."

"Maybe," DiBella said. "We could shake Animal a little, see what came out."

"We can always do that," I said. "If we do it too soon and release him, he'll be looking for whoever ratted him out, and no one will talk to me again."

"You figure Wendell and the Clark kid hooked up somehow, and Grant got the guns from Animal."

"Yeah." I said. "And Animal had taught Grant how to shoot, and, maybe, for whatever reason, Grant taught Clark."

"That would make it sort of not spur of the moment," DiBella said.

"It would," I said.

"No surprise," DiBella said. "Part of the excitement of something like this is probably the planning and preparation."

"So," I said. "They decide to do the shooting. They buy guns and ammo from Animal. They practice until they're ready. And off they go."

"Yeah?"

"So," I said, "assuming Animal didn't give them the guns and ammo because he's a generous guy, where'd they get the money?"

"Families are well off," DiBella said. "Hell, the Clark family is loaded."

"'Hey, Dad, gimme a couple grand to buy guns and ammo'?"

"Good point," DiBella said. "Find out when either or both came up with a chunk of cash, and you got an idea when the gun deal went down."

"Yep."

"Still don't excite me," DiBella said. "We got the shooters. We got their confessions. Los Diablos are Boston's problem, and I'm not sure Animal is a major threat to civil order in Bethel County."

"Animal is small change," I said. "But I still want to know why."

"And you think if you know why, you'll be able to clear the Clark kid?" DiBella said.

"I won't know that until I know why," I said.

DiBella nodded thoughtfully.

"I don't know how smart you are," he said. "But I'll give you stubborn."

"May be better than smart," I said.

"May be," DiBella said. "Both is even better."

Pearl exhausted the yogurt carton and abandoned the remnants. She came and sat next to me and looked hopeful.

"So," DiBella said. "Fine. Go to it. But pick up the chewed carton first."

Which I did. A man's only as good as his word.

28

I SAT WITH Lily Ellsworth in a large, domed-glass conservatory with a view of the Bethel River, which moved in big blue meanders across the floor of the Bethel Valley under the high, cloudless sky.

"What have you to report?" she said.

"I think he probably did it," I said.

"I didn't hire you to tell me he did it," Mrs. Ellsworth said.

"Yes, ma'am," I said.

She sat very straight in her chair, her hands clasped motionless in her lap. She was perfectly groomed and perfectly still. Under her careful makeup, her skin had a healthy, outdoorsy look to it. Her hair was white, not silver, but white, and brushed back softly off her face. She was quite beautiful.

"Did you ever give money to your grandson?" I said.

"Often," she said.

"Large amounts?" I said.

"What might seem a large amount to you," she said, "might seem a very small amount to me."

I nodded. I did the math in my head.

"Two or three thousand dollars?" I said.

"I have given him that much."

"Often?"

"No, last winter," she said. "He needed it."

"Did he say what for?"

"No," she said. "And I did not ask. I love my grandson, Mr. Spenser."

I nodded.

"Can you recall exactly when last winter?" I said.

"Not really."

"Did you write a check?"

"Yes."

"Could you look it up?" I said.

"Why is that necessary?"

"I believe he bought some guns with the money," I said. "It might help to know when."

"He did not buy guns," she said.

"Ma'am," I said. "They already have him cold. Grant has named him as the other shooter. He's confessed to it. I don't have to help convict him. Anything I can find out will be useful only on his behalf."

"Or you won't use it?" she said.

"Correct," I said.

She nodded slowly. We looked out through the glass at the slow lawn that declined toward the valley. Along one side was a stand of hydrangea, their big blossoms moving in the soft wind.

"It is four-ten in the afternoon," she said. "Would you care for a cocktail?"

"That would be nice," I said.

She stood effortlessly and walked briskly out of the glass room. I watched the hydrangea blossoms move for a while. She came back with a tray with two glasses on it.

"Gin and tonic," she said. "I suppose I should have asked."

"That will be fine," I said.

She set the tray down on a low table, and I saw that her checkbook was on the tray also. She handed me one of the glasses and took the other for herself. She raised it toward me slightly.

"You seem an honest man, sir," she said.

"'Let be be the end of seem,'" I said.

She smiled faintly.

"'The only emperor,'" she said, "'is the emperor of ice-cream.'"

"Very good," I said.

"My generation read, Mr. Spenser; apparently yours did, too."

"Or at least I did," I said. "Still do."

"Yes," she said. "I do as well."

She took another pull at her drink. Then she put the glass down, picked up the checkbook, and began to leaf through the register. I sat with my drink. The hydrangea continued to nod in the late summer outside the glass.

"I gave him three thousand dollars on January twenty-first," she said after a time. "How many guns would that buy?"

"Four plus ammo," I said. "And he might have had some left over."

"For ski masks," she said.

"And extra magazines," I said. "Perhaps even a controlled substance."

"Drugs?"

I shrugged.

"I believe none of this," she said.

"No need to yet," I said.

"Nothing will make me believe it."

I didn't speak.

"You believe it," she said.

"I think it likely," I said.

"And you think when he bought the guns in January, he was planning to shoot those people in May."

"I don't know when he was planning to shoot," I said. "I only know when he got the money and when he did the shooting."

"He didn't do the shooting."

"Have you talked to him since the incident?" I said.

"Yes."

"Did you ever ask?"

"No."

"Excuse me, ma'am, for saying so, but you don't want to know."

She looked at her drink, tilting the glass slightly so the ice rattled faintly.

"Jared has always been a silent child," she said. "Perhaps lonely. I don't know. I always felt that everyone pried at him too much. His parents were always after him to tell them more. Where are you going? Who are you going with? Who are your friends? Do you have a girlfriend? What do you wish to become? I felt my role was to offer him respite, a place he could come and be loved and respected, where he could indulge himself in as much silence as he wished."

"Did you spend much time with him?"

"A great deal of time."

"Did he have a girlfriend?" I said.

"I don't know," she said. "Nor do I know about friends or ambitions or fears or hopes and dreams."

"What did you talk about?"

"Books, movies, ideas."

"Ideas?" I said.

She smiled.

"We talked about love," she said. "We talked about friendship. We talked about what humans should be. About what one human owed another. About what made a person good."

"But in the abstract," I said.

"Yes."

"Without concrete examples," I said.

"None tied to him," she said.

"Better than not talking about them at all," I said.

"Yes."

"Did you have any sense that some of these issues might have a personal connection?" I said.

"I never pried."

"Could you give a guess," I said.

She was quiet, looking at her glass. Then she raised it and took a long swallow.

"I would guess," she said, "that they did."

29

THE STOREFRONT wasn't lit very well, and was kind of gloomy. I took some time for my eyes to adjust while I looked around. Next to the door was an old-fashioned Coke cooler, the red paint faded and along the edges chipped away. There was a deeply tarnished bottle-cap opener screwed to the side. At the far back end of the room was a pool table with a light hanging over it, the felt surface of the table a patch of bright green under the light. Some folding chairs and card tables were set around the room, and on the left side, there was a big, yellow oak desk and an expensive leather swivel chair with a high back and a padded headrest. There were a few men playing cards at a couple of the tables. A tall, sharp-edged, quick-looking man in a bright white tuxedo shirt sat in the swivel chair with his feet up on the desk. He was black. So was everyone else in the room. They all looked at me silently when I came in. I felt whiter than Mr. Clean.

The lean, hard guy at the desk studied me as I came in. I stood and let him look. Nobody said anything. A radio somewhere was playing rap music, but not so loud that I couldn't stand it.

The guy in the swivel chair said, "Jesus Christ."

"Almost," I said.

"Spenser," the guy said.

"Major," I said.

"You looking for me?" Major said.

"I am," I said.

"So?"

I hooked an empty folding chair and walked with it to the desk. I put it down and sat on it.

A short, thick man with prison tattoos and no hair spoke to Major.

"You want fish flop out of here?" he said.

Major shook his head.

"Know him, long time ago," Major said. "Him and Hawk."

"Some of my best friends are black," I said.

The thick man stared at me. I bore up as best I could. After a while, he sat down. But he kept looking.

"I sense racial intolerance," I said to Major.

"You better fucking believe it," Major said. "What you want here?"

"Need some help," I said.

"From motherfucking me?"

"Beautifully put," I said.

Major almost smiled.

"What you need?" he said.

"You still in the gang business?"

"Not me," Major said. "I president of the Chamber of Commerce."

"And you owe it all to me and Hawk," I said.

"Sho 'nuff. Set me on the path to re-fucking-demption."

"Makes me proud," I said.

"So what you want?"

"I'm interested in a Boston gang calls itself Los Diablos," I said.

Major laughed.

"The fucking Fritos," he said. "What you want with Losfucking-Diablos."

"Need to talk with a guy named Jose Yang."

"Chink Frito," Major said. "He runs the thing."

"Where do they operate?" I said.

"Where we fucking let them," Major said.

"We?"

Major grinned at me.

"Hobart Chamber of Commerce," he said. "Major Johnson, head nigger."

"So where do you let them operate?"

"Part of Dorchester," Major said. "What you want with them."

"Yang's got a younger brother, Animal, involved in something I'm working on out in the far western suburbs."

"Animal?" Major said. "The bodybuilder?"

I nodded.

"Out in the white, white west?" Major said.

"Yes."

"Animal dumber than my dick?" Major said.

"Big and scary, though," I said. "Reminds me a little of John Porter."

"John Porter in the ground, man. Long time."

"Somebody shoot him?"

" 'Course they did, man. What you think?"

"Can you set me up with Yang?" I said.

"I want to," Major said. "I can."

I nodded.

"What you want to do with him," Major said. "I can have somebody dart him, you want."

"No. His brother maybe supplied the guns used in that big school shootout last spring."

"And you want to know if Chink Frito supply them. Say he do. What you gonna do then?"

"Nothing right away," I said. "I'm just gathering information."

"And what you do if Jose don't like you asking, and decide to deuce yo' white ass?"

"I figure you won't let him."

Major sat back in the big, expensive swivel chair and looked at me, beginning to smile. I hadn't seen him in more than twelve years. He'd been a kid then. Now he was probably in his early thirties, and he looked like Tommy Hearns. His eyes were bright with intelligence and scorn and anger, as they had been. But there was control in them, too, instead of the craziness. Hawk had said a long time ago that Major Johnson was more like Hawk than most people.

"You got some big bangers," he said, "for a Bud Light. You see Hawk around?"

"Often," I said.

"Tell him I say hello," Major said.

"You want to set up my meeting with Jose Yang?" I said.

"Sure," Major said.

30

WITH PEARL ASLEEP in the backseat, I pulled into the parking lot at the country store in the late afternoon, and sat with the motor running and the a/c on low. In maybe five minutes, a vast Chevy Suburban pulled up beside me and Janey got out. I rolled down my window.

"Thanks for coming," she said. "I didn't know who else to call."

"Nice vehicle," I said.

"Oh, the car, that's Daddy's. We have horses."

"They ride in the backseat?" I said.

She smiled faintly.

"George's in the car," Janey said. "Animal beat her up."

"Can she move around?" I said.

"Yes."

"Okay, put her in my front seat. You get in back with Pearl."

"She's scrunched down in the front seat," Janey said. "She's afraid Animal will see her."

"I'll take care of her," I said.

Janey nodded.

When George got out of the car, she moved very carefully, as if her ribs hurt. She had one eye swollen shut and a fat lip and a long welt along her jawline. She eased herself into my front seat, and Janey closed the door behind her carefully and got in back. Without raising her head, Pearl opened her eyes and growled. Janey froze.

"I don't think she'll bite you," I said.

"You don't think?"

I reached back and patted Pearl's head.

"You pat, too," I said.

Janey did, cautiously. Pearl stopped growling. Her short tail wagged.

"Easy," I said.

I looked at George. She had cowered down into the corner of the front seat.

"How are you?" I said.

"I don't know," she said.

"In pain?"

"I'm real sore," she said.

"I'm going to take you to the emergency room," I said. "They'll give you something to feel better."

"I can't go to no hospital," George said. "Animal said I went to a hospital or anything, he'd kill me."

"He won't," I said.

I put the car in drive and pulled out onto the street.

"He beat her up for talking to you," Janey said from the backseat. "Somebody saw us at the mall."

"He said he was going to kill me if he ever saw us together again."

"You tell him what we talked about?" I said.

"I said you was asking about Jared Clark, but I didn't tell you nothing," she said.

She mumbled some because her lip was so fat.

"He's gonna kill me," she said.

"No," I said. "He's not."

"He'll find out," she said.

"He's not going to hurt you," I said.

"How you gonna stop him?" she said. "You can't stay with me all the time."

"Parents?" I said.

She made a noise.

"Shit," she said.

So much for parents. At the hospital, Janey stayed in the car with Pearl. I went in with George and waited while they cleaned her up. When he was through with her, the young emergency-room doctor came out to talk with me.

"You her father?" he said.

"No. Friend of a friend."

"Well," he said. "She'll be okay. No broken bones. I don't think anything wrong internally. She's scared to death and in some discomfort."

"You give her something?"

"Yes. Three days' worth."

"She tell you she uses drugs?" I said.

"No, but I assumed. I didn't give her a prescription."

"Any limits on what she should do?"

"She should stay away from whoever hit her," the doctor said. "Otherwise, just rest."

"I'll see to both," I said.

"You know who did it?" the doctor said.

"Yes."

"We'll have to report this to the police," the doctor said. "It's an obvious beating."

"I know."

"We'll need your name for the police," the doctor said. He smiled a little. "And she has no medical insurance."

I took out one of my cards and gave it to him.

"Send me the bill," I said.

31

WE DROPPED JANEY OFF near the Coffee Nut, and George and I and Pearl went back to Boston to my place.

"You want to call your parents?" I said.

"Naw."

"They won't be wondering where you are?" I said.

"Naw."

"You have parents," I said.

"Sort of."

"You live at home?"

"Sometimes."

It wasn't going anywhere, so I decided to drop it.

"Okay, you'll stay here until I have squared things to Animal," I said.

"How you gonna do that?"

"Vigorously," I said. "Take the bedroom."

"You gonna have sex with me?" she said.

"Nope."

"Why not?"

"Too young," I said.

"I know how," she said.

"Good to have a skill," I said.

"I done it a lot."

"Practice makes perfect," I said.

"You don't wanna?"

"I'm flattered to be asked," I said. "But my heart belongs to another."

"You gonna let me stay here for nothing?"

"That's what I'm going to do," I said.

I took the couch. It was a big, comfortable couch, but it was less convenient than it sounded, because Pearl also took the couch, and my first night there was not very restful. Nor was Pearl's.

In the morning, George was moving better. She emerged late, wearing one of my shirts for a nightgown. It was sufficiently modest. The shirttails reached her knees. I made us breakfast and left her to eat it, and Pearl to watch her, while I went into my bathroom for a shower and then to my bedroom for clean clothes. By the time I came out, freshly scrubbed and clean shaven, she had finished breakfast. I noticed that she hadn't eaten too much. She took out a pack of cigarettes and lit one. I disapproved, but I figured this wasn't the week for her to quit, so I just opened one window a crack in the living room, and didn't comment.

I didn't want to leave her alone yet, so I sat and read

David McCullough's book on John Adams while she was in the bedroom with the television going. We didn't have much to say, so we didn't say it. She slept a lot. I made her some soup. At supper, I asked her a few questions about Jared Clark that she didn't know the answers to. I was pretty sure that we could make a very long list of questions she wouldn't know the answer to. After supper, Pearl and I watched the Sox game on the living-room television and spent a second night on the couch in territorial conflict.

The next morning, when George came out she was wearing another of my shirts, but her hair was combed and she looked like she'd washed. She was moving pretty well, and she didn't seem either pained or drugged. After breakfast, I showed her how to operate my washer-dryer, and she put her clothes through. While she was doing that, I checked my answering machine at the office. There was a message from Major Johnson. I wrote down the details.

Late in the afternoon, fully dressed in her laundered clothes, George came into the living room, smoking a cigarette.

"I'm bored," she said.

"Me, too."

She looked startled, as if it hadn't occurred to her that I might experience anything.

"How long I gotta stay here?"

"Long as you think you need to," I said.

"I gotta hide from Animal."

"Doesn't mean you can't go out and walk around," I said. "It's a big city."

"What are you going to do?"

"Got some business tonight," I said. "How you feeling?"

"I feel okay."

The bruise along her jawline was now blue and yellow, and the swollen eye had opened a little. Her lip was still fat. I went to the kitchen and got a spare set of keys from what Susan called the "crap drawer," where I kept such things. The name seemed harsh to me.

"You want to go out," I said. "Big key opens the front door downstairs. Other one opens my door. Pearl should stay in until I get back."

"I never been in Boston before," she said.

"Of course not," I said. "It must be forty miles."

"I never been anywhere," she said.

I wrote my address and home phone number on the back of one of my business cards and gave it to her.

"You get lost, take a cab back here," I said. "Or you call me."

"I don't have any money," she said.

Of course she didn't.

I gave her some.

32

·

THE SOUTH BAY SHOPPING MALL was tucked in under Southampton Street, just west of Andrew Square across the expressway. It was dark when I got there and met Major Johnson in front of the Home Depot. There were a number of other youngish black men with Major, and none of them seemed impressed with me.

"So," Major said. "Whitefish, wha's happenin'."

"'Wha's happenin'?'" I said. "I keep telling you, Major, you African guys aren't going to integrate with our culture if you insist on talking funny."

"Fuck you," Major said.

"There you go," I said. "White guys say that to me, too."

Major grinned at me suddenly.

"I forgot what you was like," he said.

"How could you," I said. "Jose arrive yet?"

"He be along," Major said. "Gonna meet us over there by the fence, where the tracks are."

"Why don't I go over and wait for him?" I said.

"No. Tole him he could come in first, set up like he wanted. We'd walk in on him."

"Make him feel secure," I said.

"Sho'," Major said.

"He know about me?" I said.

"Knows there a honkie muthafucka wants to talk with him."

"Think he'll recognize me?"

Major grinned again.

"As opposed to all the other honkie muthafuckas that be with us?" he said.

"Good point," I said. "You'll know when he gets here?"

"We'll know," Major said.

The stores had started to close and a lot of people had left the parking lot when Jose Yang showed up. A smallish coffee-colored kid with tattoos and cornrows came across the lot and spoke to Major.

"He here," the kid said.

Major turned and looked at the rest of his crew. He didn't say anything, but they moved as if he had, fanning out as they moved across the parking lot toward the railroad fence.

"Le's go," Major said to me.

There was no concealment in the parking lot. It was brightly lit and sparsely occupied. By the fence at the far side, I could see two cars parked side by side, parallel to the fence, their noses pointed toward Southampton Street. As we walked, people got out of the cars and stood behind them. Major's crew was now fanned out around them in a semi-circle. They stopped about fifty feet from the cars. Major and I kept walking.

When we were maybe twenty feet away, one of the men behind the cars said, "Stop there."

We stopped. We all looked at one another. The man who had spoken was more Asian-looking than Animal, but I could see the familial connection. He was shorter than Animal, with sloping shoulders and longish arms. His black hair was long. He wore a sleeveless T-shirt, and both his thick arms were heavily tattooed.

"You want to talk with me, Snowflake?" he said.

"More racial animosity," I said to Major.

"Nobody like you people," Major said. "You got to un-nerstand that."

"It's so unfair," I said.

"You want to talk or not," the guy with the tattoos said.

"You Jose Yang?" I said.

"Yeah."

"My name's Spenser."

I was hoping the name would strike fear into Los Diablos.

"So what?" Yang said.

Beside me, Major Johnson snickered.

"I know your brother," I said. "Animal."

"So?"

"I need to know if you got him some handguns," I said.

"Why you need to know that?" Yang said.

"I'm a private detective," I said. "I'm working on a case. It won't involve Animal."

"How I know that?" Yang said.

"He say something," Major said, "it be true."

"You say so," Yang said to Major.

"I do. He say something, you can take it right down the First National Bank of Cha-Cha and deposit it."

Yang nodded.

"I don't know nothing about no guns," he said to me.

"Would have been last January," I said. "Four clean pieces and ammo."

"Why I tell you shit?" Yang said.

"I tole him you would," Major said.

Yang looked hard at him across the hood of the Chevy Impala he was behind. Major waited. Yang was silent. Behind him, the two carloads of backup stood silently. I spotted at least a shotgun among them. I didn't know for sure what else. They stayed behind the cars. I had no idea what kind of ordnance Major's people had broken out. They were behind us, and I didn't want to violate the moment by turning to look. Far behind me was the sound of traffic on the expressway. In the parking lot, I could hear car doors open and slam, and car engines start up, as late shoppers and store employees headed home.

"You trust him?" Yang said to Major.

"Man do what he say he do," Major said. "Like me."

Yang nodded. More staring. More traffic sounds. One of Yang's men coughed and tried to stifle it. We waited.

"My brother got big muscles and no brain," Yang said.

"Some question about the size of his cojones, too," I said.

"Yeah," Yang said. "I know. Why I sent him out there to East Cow Fuck."

"Last January," I said.

"A Browning, a Colt, two Glocks," Yang said. "No history, extra magazines, lotta bullets."

"How much?" I said.

"Fifteen hundred," Yang said. "The works."

"Cheap," I said.

"He's my brother," Yang said. "I didn't make no profit."

"He did," I said. "He had three grand to spend."

Yang was silent for a moment, then he said, "That would be Luis."

"He say what the guns were for?"

"No."

"They were used in a bunch of murders out in Dowling."

"You ain't involving my brother," Yang said.

"Not if I don't have to."

"You rat him," Yang said, "I kill you."

"I don't want him," I said. "I'll do what I can."

"You better do it," Yang said.

"Don't be threatening my man," Major said.

"Major, you and me already lived longer than we was supposed to." Yang's voice was flat. "I said what I said."

"You fuck with my man," Major said, "and we see 'bout that."

"I ain't heavy," I said. "I'm his brother."

Major choked off a laugh beside me. Yang gave me a hard look, and then it was over. Our side backed down toward the Home Depot. Yang's side got in their cars and drove out the Southampton Street exit.

33

"HEALY SAYS I CAN bend things a little for you," Di-Bella told me as he parked his car behind a couple of state highway maintenance buildings off the Mass Pike near Worcester. One was an open-front garage where they stored salt and sand for the winter. We went in and found Animal Yang behind the salt pile with two mean-looking state troopers.

"Here he is," DiBella said.

Animal had on a black Nike Dri Fit muscle shirt and looked impressive.

"We took a piece off him," one of the troopers said. He held up a short Beretta .380.

"Hang on to it," DiBella said.

He looked at Animal. "Got a permit?"

Animal shook his head. DiBella looked at me.

"Want us to run the piece for you?"

I shook my head.

"Unload it and give it back to him," I said.

The trooper who held Animal's gun looked at DiBella. He was a big black guy with no hair visible under his campaign hat.

"I told you," DiBella said to him, "when I called you. This is all off the record. If anyone asks you about it, it never happened."

The black trooper shrugged, took the magazine out of the handle, and put it in his pocket, ejected the round from the chamber, let it lie on the floor where it landed, and handed the gun back to Animal. Animal took it and held it as if he didn't know what to do with it.

"Okay," DiBella said to the troopers, "you boys beat it. I owe you one."

"Maybe two or three," the black trooper said.

They went.

"I'll be in the car," DiBella said.

He went after them. I was alone with Animal.

"You suckered me out by the lake," Animal said. "Don't mean you can do it again."

I hit him with a left hook that staggered him back against the salt pile.

"Does too," I said.

I took my gun off my hip and pressed the barrel of it hard into the recess under his cheekbone below the left eye.

"Ow," Animal said. "That hurts."

"I know," I said.

"Whaddya fucking want with me," he said.

"I'm thinking about killing you," I said.

"I never done nothing to you," he said.

I kept pressing the gun. He was sweating and his face was pale. I knew it hurt, and I knew he was scared. Which was the way it was supposed to be.

"That cop'll hear you if you shoot," Animal said.

"Like he'll care," I said.

"Ow, man, that really hurts, man," Animal said.

"Like I care," I said.

"Don't do it, man," Animal said. "I didn't do nothing to you. Gimme a break. Don't do it."

He was stiff against the discomfort of the gun barrel.

"You beat up George," I said.

"Who?"

"George, one of your girlfriends."

"I just gave her a couple whacks, man. You . . . ow, man, that hurts, man . . . ease it up, man, please. I didn't do nothing!"

"You got one miserable chance to live," I said.

"Man, I'll do whatever you say. Ow, man. Stop it."

"If you ever touch her again," I said, "I'll kill you on sight. I'll find you and I'll kill you."

I twisted the gun barrel a little. He groaned.

"You understand?" I said.

"Yeah, man, I'll never touch her. I promise you, I'll never go near her."

"If anything happens, if somebody you don't know

bumps into her on his bicycle and knocks her down, anything. I will find you and shoot you into little fucking pieces."

"Man, I'll never hurt her, I promise. I promise. I won't let
no one else hurt her. Honest to God, I won't."

I took the gun away from his face and held it at my side.
He put both hands up to his face to rub the sore spot, and
realized he was still holding the empty Beretta, and dropped
it on the floor and pressed his hands against his face. He
started to cry.

"You got the guns from your brother," I said.

"Wha?"

"I talked with him, your brother Jose. He sold you the
four guns for fifteen hundred dollars. You sold them to the
two kids for three thousand dollars."

"What kids?"

I slapped him hard with my left hand.

"Grant and Clark," I said. "One or both."

"Grant asked me. Clark kid had the dough."

"And you taught them to shoot," I said.

"Yeah."

I brought my gun up suddenly and fired into the salt a foot
to the left of his head. He screamed. I fired into the salt a
foot to the right of him. He doubled up, screaming, "No, no,
no, no, no."

"Don't you even look at that girl again," I said. "Ever."

I put my gun away and walked out of the garage.

"You shoot him?" DiBella said.

"No," I said.

"Probably should have," DiBella said.

I nodded.

"Probably," I said.

34

I DROPPED GEORGE in Dowling Center. "I'll drive you home," I said.

She shook her head.

"Might be a good place to sort of crash a little while," I said.

She shook her head again.

"And you're sure Animal won't get me?"

"He won't," I said.

She got out of the car and lingered for a moment on the sidewalk with the car door open. Her bruises had started to yellow. Her lip was down. She was looking better.

"Thanks for, like, helping me," she said.

"You're welcome," I said.

She took my card out of the pocket of her jeans and looked at it for a moment.

"Call me if you need me," I said.

She nodded and looked again at my card.

"Bye," she said.

"Bye."

She closed the car door and turned and walked away, still holding my card in her hand. I watched her until she turned the corner past the town green and disappeared behind the Town Hall. Then I pulled away and found a parking spot near the Coffee Nut and parked and went in to see if the gang was around.

They were.

"Hey," Janey said as I came in.

She was sitting with her friend of the white top, whose name turned out to be Erika, and Carly Simon, looking crisp in a green polo shirt and tan shorts.

"Coffee?" he said, and nodded at the empty seat in the booth.

I sat. Other kids in other booths looked at me covertly. Animal had made my rep, bless his heart.

"Is George, like, okay?" Janey said.

"She's fine," I said. "Animal has promised me that he won't bother her again."

"You shake him up again?" Carly said.

There was in his voice an implication of shared knowledge, as though he had shaken up a few people in his time, too. I smiled. I had known Major Johnson when he was only a little older than Carly. Different planets.

"We reasoned together," I said. "Talk to me a little more about Jared Clark."

"What's to tell," Carly said. "He didn't bother us; we, you know, didn't bother him."

"Did he get bullied much?" I said.

The girls both deferred to Carly. It's good to be a football hero.

"No," Carly said. "Like, he didn't play ball or nothing, and he didn't joke around, and most of the time, he wasn't, like, even around. But nobody bothered him much."

Carly looked at Erika and Janey.

"You think?" he said.

"No," Erika said. "He was just, like, around, and nobody really noticed him much."

"Girlfriend?" I said.

Janey shook her head as she thought about it.

"I mean, he never asked anybody out," she said. "That I know about. Erika, you know anybody?"

"Nope."

Erika had longish nails with the tips painted white, and she admired them unconsciously while she spoke.

"I suppose he might have hooked up with one of the loser girls, you know?" Erika said. "But we wouldn't know that anyway. None of them hang with us."

"Was Jared a loser?" I said.

Janey thought about the question carefully. Evidently, loser was a precisely defined category.

"Well," Janey said, "no, not exactly, I guess. I mean, he was shy and everything. And he wasn't popular, but he wasn't a geek. He was like more of a loner."

"But people weren't actively cruel to him?"

All three of them shook their heads.

"How about Wendell Grant?" I said.

"He played ball," Carly said.

"Any good?" I said.

Carly shrugged.

"He was okay," Carly said. "Big, you know. Took up a lot of room. But he was really dumb. Couldn't remember the plays. And clumsy. Coach designed a sweep right for me behind Dell, and Dell could never pull and get out there. He, like, messed it up every time. Coach finally forgot about it."

"Was he dumb in school?"

"Oh, you better believe it," Erika said. "He was in my geometry class and he called that guy from olden times— you know, Pythagoras. He called him Py-tha-gor-us, and we all, like, broke up, you know? Even Mrs. Root couldn't keep from laughing. Dell was pissed."

"That sort of thing happen a lot?" I said.

Erika shrugged.

"We all thought he was pretty dumb," Janey said.

"He useta carry a knife," Carly said. "You know, one of those big hunting jackknifes."

"A buck knife," I said.

"Yeah. Like that. Comes in a little leather case?"

I nodded.

"He ever use it?" I said.

"Naw. He useta flash it around a lot when there was no teachers. But that's all."

"He date much?" I said.

"Ick!" Janey said.

"That would be a no?" I said.

"He was creepy," Janey said.

"Like?"

"Like, you know he'd say stuff. . . ."

"Hey," Erika said, imitating a boy, "you girls like it rough?"

"Did he play rough."

"He was the kind of guy, you're standing in line in the cafeteria and he's rubbing up against you, trying to get a feel," Janey said.

"Yeah, one of those guys *accidentally* bumps your boob with his elbow," Erika said, making quote signs with her forefingers around "accidentally."

"And he was always talking about fighting and guns," Janey said, "and, you know, like, how tough he was."

"Was he?"

Again, the girls deferred to Carly. He shrugged.

"He's big, but, like, he's a fucking buffoon, you know? Nobody was scared of him, 'cept a few pussies he could pick on. Guys on the team told him fuck off."

"Did he pick on Jared?" I said.

"Not that I seen," Carly said.

"He hung out at the Rocks?"

"Yeah," Carly said. "Animal was his freaking hero."

"You surprised he shot up the school?" I said.

"Hell, yes," Carly said. "I didn't think he had the balls, you know?"

"How about Jared," I said.

Carly shrugged. He looked at the two girls. They shook their heads. He shook his head.

"He didn't seem the type," Carly said.

"He was just, like, going about his business," Janey said.

"He tight with Grant?"

"Him and Dell? No," Janey said. "I never saw them hanging, you?"

Erika said, "No." Carly shook his head.

"Jared get along with the faculty?" I said.

"I don't know," Carly said.

"I never heard about him getting in trouble," Erika said. "I think he's seen Miss Blair a couple times. She's, you know, the guidance lady."

"I know," I said. "You know why he saw her?"

"Oh, Christ," Janey said. "They send you to see Blair if you're late twice. Make sure you don't have, like, a fucking emotional problem."

"You've seen her?"

"Sure. I told her I didn't have a problem. The school had a problem, it was fucking borrrrrring."

We all laughed.

"I remember it well," I said.

35

I WENT TO SEE Chief Cromwell in his office at Dowling Police headquarters. DiBella had called ahead for me, so they wouldn't open fire when I arrived. But I still had to wait a long time at the front desk. I was willing to. And finally, they sent me on in.

Cromwell mad-dogged me for a while, giving me the dead-eye cop stare he was working on. I moved a chair a little closer to his desk and sat down and crossed my legs.

"Hi," I said.

Cromwell stared some more.

"How ya doin'?" I said.

More staring. Then, when he had me softened up, he spoke.

"You just won't learn," Cromwell said.

"I can't," I said. "Nobody tells me anything."

"What do you want to know, for crissake. We got the killers. They've confessed. What the fuck are you after?"

"I know where they got the guns," I said.

"Yeah?"

"And how they got the money to buy them."

"Yeah?"

"You ever have any complaints about either of them?" I said.

"Clark or Grant?"

"Yes."

Cromwell leaned back in his chair. I noticed the pearl-handled .45 was back in its shiny holster on the corner of his desk. Looked good there.

"Well," Cromwell said after a while. "I can't talk you out of this, and I can't seem to scare you off."

"You could try charming me," I said.

"Would that work?"

"No, but I wouldn't have to punch you in the balls."

He rocked his spring-loaded swivel a little.

"Nobody wants this opened up," he said after a while. "The kids' parents, the school, the kids themselves."

He looked at me heavily for a minute.

"I don't. Town doesn't. We want to wrap it up neat and put it away and get on with it."

"How 'bout the people who lost someone in the shooting?" I said.

"They want it over. They know we got the bastards. They want to see them fry, and they want to move on as best they can. Nobody wants you opening up all the fucking wounds again."

"They won't fry in this state," I said.

"I know, just a manner of speaking," he said. "Been simpler if we'd shot them dead on the spot."

"That would have required you all to actually go on in there and maybe interrupt things," I said.

Cromwell nodded slowly. All of the General Patton crap seemed to have drained from him. He seemed gray and tired, almost human.

"I know," he said. "I know."

"You didn't know what to do," I said, "did you."

He shook his head.

"We're a small town," he said. "Upper-class. Quiet. We never ran into this sort of thing. Most of my guys never fired their weapons except on the range."

"You?" I said.

He looked at the big six-gun on the corner of his desk as if he'd never seen it before.

"No," he said.

"Hard to learn on the job like that," I said. "Most people aren't ready the first time."

"God, I hope there's no second time," he said.

"There'll be something," I said. "Sometime. And you'll be more ready."

"You're not going to leave this alone," Cromwell said.

"No," I said. "I'm not. Either of these kids got a history with you?"

"I don't give out juvie files," he said.

"I'm not looking for files. Just information. You and me.

Alone in the room. Either of them been in trouble you know about?"

"We talked to the Grant kid couple times," Cromwell said.

He was looking past my left shoulder, out an office window, at the nice, neat stretch of lawn in front of the station. Orderly.

"He was shooting cats with a pellet gun," Cromwell said slowly. "Strays mostly, but he got a couple pets and the owners complained and we brought him in and talked with him and his mother. He was maybe thirteen." He shook his head.

"I've met his mother," I said.

"She just sort of said the hell with him. Like he's some sort of aberration. It's not my fault."

"Talk to his grandfather?" I said.

"They begged us not to. Both of them. I felt bad for the kid, tell you the truth. His mother's just a waste of time."

"The last hippie," I said.

"Yeah," Cromwell said. "So we confiscated the pellet gun and told him he was on probation and we were giving him a break, so if he got in any more trouble, we'd go hard on him."

"Did he?"

"Nothing official. I heard he hung out at the Rocks with the burnouts and freaks. But we never had any reason to bring him in again."

"What'd you do with the pellet gun?" I said.

"Give it to my sister's kid, lives outside Stockbridge."

"And he probably uses it to shoot cats," I said.

Cromwell shrugged.

"Maybe," he said. "But he's not doing it here."

"Anything with Jared Clark?"

"No. Never even heard of him until the Grant kid fingered him after the shooting."

"Ever talk with anybody about him?" I said.

"Talked with the school shrink."

"Dr. Blair?"

"Yeah. You met her?"

I nodded.

"She's something, isn't she?"

"She is," I said. "What did she tell you?"

"Classic stuff," Cromwell said. "Jared was bullied a lot. Kids picked on him. Pushed him around. She feels he allied himself with Grant so that Grant would protect him."

"Why would Grant protect him?" I said.

"Don't know. He was the school tough guy. Big kid. Football player. Who would have thought it, him having the mother he did?"

"Sometimes, I guess, the apple falls as far as it can from the tree," I said.

He nodded.

"You know of any previous connection between Clark and Grant?" I said.

"No. But, you know how it is, they don't pop up on the screen unless they are causing trouble."

"And these guys weren't?"

"Except for the cat killings," Cromwell said.

"Love to know how they got together," I said.

"Maybe Blair knows," Cromwell said. "Ask her. Be a good excuse to talk with her."

"I will," I said. "Maybe she'll show me her knees."

"You gonna tell me about where they got the guns?" Cromwell said.

"No," I said.

"Isn't that sort of like withholding evidence?" Cromwell said.

"It's not like you need it for a conviction," I said.

Cromwell nodded.

"Just thought I'd ask," he said.

36

IT HAD BEEN a wet summer. Outside my office window, it was raining again. I was watching it. Pearl was resting on her couch. Later, when the excitement died down, I might read the paper. My phone rang. Pearl had no reaction. She didn't care about phones. I didn't, either, but somebody had to answer, so I picked it up.

AN HOUR LATER, Pearl and I pulled up in front of the Dowling village market. The rain was steady but not abusive. Through the steady sweep of the wipers, I saw him in front of the market, the red-haired kid from the Rocks. He was pressed against the front of the building, trying to stay dry. He was wearing the zippered top of a warm-up suit, his cap on backward, and sucking on a cigarette. His jeans were baggy, and his sneakers were black Keds high-tops. Retro. When he got in the front seat, Pearl growled at him from the back.

"What's wrong with him?" the kid said.

"Her," I said. "She doesn't like you."

"She bite?"

"Not today," I said.

I reached back and patted her. He hunched forward and a little sideways in the passenger seat, away from Pearl.

"Where we going," I said.

"How much is the reward?" he said.

"Depends on what you show me," I said.

"I'm going to take you where they did a lot of shooting."

"So you said. Let's go there and see what we see."

"But there's some reward."

"Absolutely," I said.

I couldn't figure out what I was going to get from this, but Spenser's Crime Buster Rule #8 is *Always look.*

We drove past the park that backed up to the Rocks, and down a narrow road that skirted the west end of the lake, and parked in a dirt turnaround next to a rutted dirt road.

"It's down this road," he said.

I nodded. We got out of the car. Pearl didn't like the rain much, but she loved the woods. She struggled with her ambivalence for a moment and then committed to the woods. I took my gun out from under my raincoat and put it in my raincoat pocket. Then I started back up the paved road we'd just driven down.

"Hey," the red-haired kid said, "where you going. It's in here."

"We'll come on it," I said, "from a different direction."

"Man, in this rain? Through the woods? We'll get soaked, everything's all wet in there."

"Different direction," I said.

Spenser's Crime Buster Rule #8a: *Don't blunder into something while you're looking.*

Pearl was bred to be a hunting dog, before she made a career change and became a lap dog. And sometimes her instincts resurfaced. She ranged far ahead of us, snuffling everything, and circled back to check with me before she ranged out again. She'd probably let me know if there was somebody in the woods.

The kid was right, the bushes and low branches were wet and pressed their wetness against us as we moved through them. But I had no way to know this wasn't a setup, and until I did, I'd have to act as if it was. But it wasn't. We came into a clearing in the woods and saw Pearl sniffing something carefully. There was no one there, no sound of anyone anywhere, nor did Pearl act as if there was anyone. I took my hand off my gun, though I left it there in my pocket. I took a look at what Pearl had found. It was the desiccated body of a dead cat.

"This is the place, man," the kid said. "I'm freakin' soaked."

The cat had been shot. I could see the shattered skull where the dry skin had receded. I could tell Pearl was considering picking it up. I told her not to. As I circled the clearing, there were other dead cats, and a shiny scatter of brass. I picked up one of the casings. It was nine-millimeter. I scuffed through the leaf meal bed of the clearing. There was more brass. Probably a couple of hundred rounds. Pearl nosed out several more cat remnants, and I had to admonish her again. There were a couple of squirrels, too. And a raccoon and some empty cat-food cans, the labels peeling off, the inside cleaned by all the squirrels and birds and bugs that had fed from them since the cans were opened.

"They come up here and shot a lot," the kid said.

He looked miserable. His sweatsuit jacket was soaked through. He was trying to smoke a damp cigarette. Because his hat was on backward, the rain drove straight into his face. But he was too fashion-conscious to turn the hat around.

"That would be Grant and Animal?"

"Yeah, and Jared, too, the other guy."

"He come with Animal and Dell?"

"I guess. I don't remember. I just know I seen him up here, too, when there was shooting."

"You watch them shoot?" I said.

"Jesus, no," he said. "You think I'm going to hang around Animal when he got a gun?"

"When did they start?"

"Last winter. They'd come up here in the freakin' snow."

I stood with my coat collar up and my hands in my pockets and looked at the clearing. Pearl, deprived of cat carcass, had gotten under the low branches of a big evergreen at the edge of the clearing and was sheltering there.

"So I get some reward?" the kid said.

I nodded.

"How much?"

"Shhhh," I said.

I kept looking. The empty cans probably meant that the cats had been lured here with cat food. The shell casings meant they had fired a lot. Some of the trees along the far edge of the clearing showed bullet scars, and a big cardboard box, now limp in the rain, looked as if it had been used as a target. I went and looked closer. It had; the crude figure of a man had been drawn on it. It was full of bullet holes. There were cardboard ammunition boxes around, faded and misshapen by long exposure. The foam interior case, where the bullets had sat, each in its own hole, was impervious to decay and would probably be there long after everyone had stopped remembering the Dowling School Massacre.

"So how much, mister? I showed you this place, huh? How much."

I got my wallet out and took five twenties and gave them to him.

"A hundred?" he said. "That's all? I thought there was a big reward."

"The big reward is for big help," I said. "I wouldn't have given you that much if it weren't raining."

"Shit, man, I'm risking my freakin' ass, Animal found out. . . ."

"Animal's not a factor," I said. "What can you tell me about Jared Clark?"

"Nothing. I didn't know him. I didn't know Dell, neither, 'cept he hung with Animal."

"But Jared didn't."

The kid shook his head.

"I just seen him come up here to shoot sometimes."

The sound of rain was different in the woods. There was no other sound competing with it, and its passage among the trees and bushes made a larger rushing sound than you heard in the city.

"Let's get out of here," I said and turned down the dirt road.

Pearl saw me move and was on her feet and moving with me. She knew the car was in that direction, and that it was dry inside the car. Her lap-dog training had kicked in.

"I don't think it's right," the kid said. "You tole me there was a reward. It ain't freakin' right I get a hundred."

"Bring me something else," I said. "Maybe I'll give you more."

We left the clearing.

RITA FIORE came into my office at lunchtime, carrying a bag of sandwiches and two cups of coffee.

"Where's your dog," she said.

"Susan has a dog walker. Pearl's with her this morning."

Rita nodded.

"I got tuna salad," she said, "on whole wheat, ham and cheese on whole wheat, egg salad on white, and pastrami on light rye."

"Excellent," I said. "Are you having anything?"

"We're sharing," she said.

"Oh."

"I want the egg salad," she said.

"I'll make do," I said.

She set everything down on my desk, took the lids off both coffees, sat down in my client chair, and unwrapped her egg-salad sandwich. I took the tuna.

"So whaddya want?" I said.

She grinned at me and crossed her legs. She was wearing a pale green linen suit with a long jacket and a short skirt.

"Same old thing," she said. "Susan's away, and I thought I might fill in."

"Would that include, say, bopping me on the couch?"

"It would," Rita said.

"You need to work on your inhibitions," I said.

"Controlling them?" Rita said.

"No," I said. "Acquiring some."

She laughed. I took a bite of my tuna sandwich.

"I take it that's another rejection?" she said.

"Sadly, yes," I said. "Where were you when I was single?"

"Prosecuting felons in Norfolk County," she said, "and keeping an eye out for Mr. Right."

"I'm not sure the Norfolk County Jail was the best place to look. No wonder you never found him," I said.

She drank some coffee and patted her lips carefully with a paper napkin.

"Actually, I've found him half a dozen times, but he never ripens well."

"'Songs unheard are sweeter far,'" I said.

"Thank you," she said. "How you doing out in Dowling."

"I am finding out more and more about less and less," I said. "I will eventually know everything about nothing."

"Like law school," she said.

"But with a better class of people," I said.

We each chewed our sandwiches and drank some coffee and used our napkins.

"I keep you talking, you may change your mind about the couch," Rita said. "Tell me what you know so far."

By the time I finished, the sandwiches were gone and the coffee was low in our cups.

"Major Johnson," she said. "Wow, that was a long time ago. How old would he be now?"

"I figure around thirty."

"And still gangbanging."

"Older gang," I said.

"Why would he help you out like that?"

"Couple of reasons. One, I'm a friend of Hawk's, and he always wanted to be like Hawk. Two, because he felt like it."

"Just because he felt like it?"

"Yes. He could, and he felt like showing that he could. Being the man is important to Major."

"So he helped you to prove he da man?" Rita said.

"Be my guess," I said.

"Is he proving it to you?"

"To me," I said. "Through me to Hawk, to Yang, to the rest of his crew, to himself. You don't know people will do what you tell them to do, unless you tell them and they do it."

"God, what a way to live," Rita said.

"It's the way he's got," I said.

"You saying he had no choice?"

I smiled and shook my head.

"I'm not navigating the nature/nurture shoals with you again," I said. "I got no idea."

"You know as well as I do," Rita said, "that whatever the

psychological reality might be, civilizations have to act as if the individual is responsible for what the individual does."

"I'd settle for knowing who was responsible for shooting up the Dowling School," I said.

Rita nodded. She finished her coffee and put the empty cup on the edge of my desk. She uncrossed her legs and recrossed them the other way.

"Perfect moment for a smoke," she said. "If we smoked. Which we don't. You could take two cigarettes from a Chinese lacquered box on your desk, and light both of them and hand one to me."

"And look you up and down insolently," I said, "through the blue smoke."

"Aladdin's lamp is mine," Rita said. "You know what strikes me about Dowling?"

"What?"

"You know they did it, but you keep right on pushing."

"I want to know why," I said.

"I would, too," Rita said. "Everything you've told me says they did it, and it was premeditated. But nothing tells me why."

"It's telling me the same thing," I said.

"There's a reason," Rita said. "I've been in the criminal law business a long time for someone as young and seductive as I am, and there's got to be a reason. Doesn't have to be a good reason. But there's got to be something."

"Uh-huh."

"And you're going to find it out."

"I am."

"You could tell the grandmother the kid did it, take your fee, and go home," Rita said. "But, of course, you won't."

"No," I said.

"Because?"

"Because I won't."

"So what's your plan?" Rita said.

"Keep pushing at it," I said.

Rita shook her head.

"You are not a quitter," she said.

"No," I said.

Rita grinned and looked at the couch.

"Me either," she said.

38

"HE WAS IN MANY WAYS the classic victim," Beth Ann Blair said. "Incommunicative, lonely, without any of the social or intellectual or athletic skills that would have made him acceptable to his peers."

"Is that why he started hanging with Dell Grant?" I said.

"I don't know. He wouldn't talk to me much. I infer from what we did talk about that he saw Dell as a protector—big football player, hung out with the tough kids from the Rocks. Jared was bullied routinely. I assume he hoped Dell would protect him."

"Did he?"

"I don't know," Beth Ann said. "I don't see these kids except in a clinical setting."

"Did he complain of it?"

"Yes, of course."

"And?" I said.

"Bullying is very difficult to prevent," Beth Ann said. "Complaining to the school authorities usually serves only to exacerbate it. I did speak to Mr. Garner on Jared's behalf, and he said he'd alert the faculty to the problem."

"Did he?"

"I'm sure he did," Beth Ann said, "but I can't speak for Mr. Garner. You'll have to ask him."

"Mr. Garner is not talking to me," I said.

Beth Ann smiled. We were in her office at the hospital, with her degrees behind her on the wall, and her lipgloss gleaming.

"He's a very resolute man," Beth Ann said. "He feels that the school, and the students in the school, which is what he cares about, are best served by putting this event behind us."

"And you?" I said.

"I'm inclined to agree. I'm not a forensic specialist, obviously, but I'm quite sure Jared is not in any legal sense insane. He may have been driven to it by loneliness and fear. He may have been victimized by bullies. He may have been corrupted by an Internet life spent in the darker corners of cyberspace. But it is hard to argue that he was not aware that what he did was wrong."

"How about an irresistible compulsion?" I said.

"No," Beth Ann said. "No, I think it was simply revenge, and however sympathetic one might be, it resulted in mass murder."

"What kind of dark corners," I said, "of the Internet."

"I'm not really sure. I know he spent a lot of time online, and the little that he would reveal to me of his inner life, he had some lurid fantasies."

"Like?"

"Violence. Dominance."

"And you feel he played those out online?"

"I know the Internet was his solace. He used to access websites that appealed to those fantasies."

"Got a name?"

"Of a website?" Beth Ann said. "No. He may have told me, but, frankly, I find them repellent."

"Porn?" I said.

"Perhaps. I did not investigate."

"How often did you see Jared?" I said.

"Not often enough, I'm afraid," Beth Ann said. "He was very reticent about getting help."

"How about Dell Grant?"

"No. I never spoke with him."

"So you don't have any theories about him."

"I can't, I'd merely be guessing."

"And what would you guess."

"No," Beth Ann said. "I won't speculate. If I had seen him enough, in a therapeutic setting, perhaps. But speculation is more about the speculator than about the, ah, patient."

"But Jared's behavior, you feel, was the result of bullying."

"Which was fed by fantasies of violent domination," Beth Ann said.

"Were the fantasies the result of the bullying?"

"I can't say. I did not have enough of him. Certainly one reinforced the other."

I nodded.

"Most of the time, there never is a clear reason," I said. "Kids do something like this. Theories are offered. None is established. Most of the time, we don't know," I said. "Do we?"

"Perhaps," Beth Ann said, "had the perpetrators spent enough time with a therapist for us to have a clear understanding of why they did it, they wouldn't have done it."

"And afterward, there's all the clutter," I said.

"Clutter?"

"People trying to justify their behavior," I said. "People trying to deal with grief. People trying to deal with rage. People trying to cover up failures. People trying to place blame. People trying to shift blame. People eager for revenge. In effect, it's done now, and we've caught the bastards. What difference does *why* make?"

"One can understand that feeling. A lot of innocent people died, for no good reason."

"We don't know what the reason was," I said. "We don't know if it was a good one or a bad one."

"There is no good reason for people to be murdered."

"Maybe not," I said. "But that's the slippery slope to abstraction. I'm just trying to find out what happened here."

"Unfortunately," Beth Ann said, "we know what happened . . . and I'm very much afraid that we'll never know why."

We both sat looking at the ground we'd replowed. Beth Ann was wearing a yellow flowered dress with ruffled shoulder straps and a low, square-cut bodice, which framed the ebb and fall of her bosom very nicely as she breathed.

"Did Jared do a lot of fantasy searches on the school computers?" I said.

"Oh." Beth Ann smiled. "Surely not. They are carefully restricted."

I nodded. Without doing anything, Beth Ann seemed to radiate sexual possibility. With Susan's absence, I was becoming steadily more preoccupied with sexual possibility, and neither Rita Fiore nor Beth Ann Blair was helping. I stood.

Beth Ann said, "You have my card."

But what I seemed to hear was *Would you like to come to my home in Lexington and have sex until the autumnal equinox?*

"Yes," I said. "I have your card."

39

THERE WAS A FOR SALE sign in front of the Clark home when Pearl and I parked in front and I got out. A sprinkler was watering the front yard to the right of the front walk. I heard the vacuum cleaner going when I came up the front walk. It shut off after I rang the bell, and in a moment, Mrs. Clark came to the front door wearing sandals and jeans and a white tank top. Her hair was done, however, and her makeup was on.

"Mr. Spenser," she said.

"I'm sorry to intrude again," I said. "But may we talk a little more?"

"Ned's not home," she said.

"You'll be just fine," I said. "I just need to ask a little more about Jared."

She didn't invite me in. But she didn't shut the door, either.

"Please leave him alone, Mr. Spenser," she said. "You can't help him. You can only make it worse. I've begged my mother to let it go. But she won't. She never does. . . ."

She shook her head hopelessly.

"Mostly I'd just like to borrow Jared's computer for a few days," I said.

"Jared didn't, doesn't, have a computer."

"Has he ever?"

"No."

"Isn't that unusual?"

"Jared was an unusual boy," Mrs. Clark said.

"Did he ever talk about being bullied?"

"No."

"Would he have told you?"

"I don't think he was being bullied," she said. "I would have known."

I nodded.

"How?" I said.

"I'm his mother," she said. "I would have known."

"And Wendell Grant?" I said. "How did he end up hanging with Wendell Grant?"

"You asked me that before," she said. "Poor Jared had too few friends for any of us to be picky about those he did have."

"So you did know Wendell?"

"No, but people, after . . . after it happened . . . they were saying, 'How could you let Jared hang around with him' . . . I didn't know, and if I did . . ."

She shrugged.

"Do you know where he would have had access to a computer?" I said.

"School, town library, places like that, I suppose. But he wouldn't have used one. I don't think he even knew how."

I was quiet. She was quiet. Somewhere next door or across the street, a dog barked. Sitting in the driver's seat of my car, Pearl barked back. Communication is a great thing. The sun shining through the languid sweep of the sprinkler made tiny rainbows in the spray.

"Please," Mrs. Clark said. "Leave him alone. Leave us alone. Jared won't even see us. We can't even live here anymore. We'll have to move and start over. Do you know, can you imagine . . . ?"

I shook my head. Tears had welled up in her eyes.

I said, "Neither of the above, Mrs. Clark. I'm sorry."

Then I went back down the walk and shooed Pearl out of the driver's seat and got in and drove away.

40

I WAS GETTING CONFLICTING STORIES, and I needed another opinion. So I was back with Jared in the Bethel County Jail. Nobody wanted me there, least of all Jared. But Healy spoke to somebody, and there I was.

"I understand a lot of kids bullied you in school," I said.

Jared shrugged.

"That true?" I said.

"No. Nobody bothered me much."

He snickered. First snicker of the day.

"Kids didn't pick on you?"

"No."

"They friendly?" I said.

"They didn't see me."

"You a loner?" I said.

"Yeah."

"You like that?" I said.

"I like being a loner," he said.

Snicker.

"I understand you were big into computers and the Internet," I said.

Jared shrugged again and snickered again.

"True?" I said.

"Computers are for losers," he said.

"You didn't use one?"

"No."

"Ever?" I said.

"No."

Snicker.

"You get along okay with Dr. Blair?" I said.

He didn't do anything, that I could see. But I had a sudden sense of something closing down.

"Sure," he said.

"You see her much?"

"Some."

"She says she couldn't help you much because you wouldn't talk to her about things," I said.

"Fuck her," Jared said.

"Did you talk with her about things?"

"Ask her," Jared said.

"I did. She says you wouldn't."

"Fuck her," he said.

I mouthed it silently along with him.

"You get along good with Dell?" I said.

"Sure."

"You like him?"

"Sure."

"Why'd you start hanging out with him?" I said.

"He was cool."

"What made him cool?" I said.

Jared shrugged.

"He was just cool," Jared said.

"How about Animal?"

Jared shrugged.

"Was Animal cool?" I said.

Jared shrugged again.

"Animal get you the guns?"

He shook his head.

"Your grandmother gave you the money," I said. "Last January. You give it to Animal?"

"I ain't ratting out nobody," Jared said.

"Why do you suppose Dr. Blair told me you were being bullied all the time and that you took refuge in nasty websites?"

"Huh?"

"Why do you suppose Dr. Blair lied about you?" I said.

"She lied about me?"

"If you're telling the truth, then she was lying."

"Fuck her," he said.

"Why do you suppose?" I said.

"'Cause she's a fucking whore, huh?"

"Why do you say that."

Jared got up and went and banged on the door. The guard opened it.

"I wanna go back to my room," he said.

"We call them cells, kid," the guard said and looked at me.

I shrugged and waved him off. The guard took him.

41

THE MESSAGE on my answering machine was simple:
"Meet me at the Rocks. Nine o'clock in the morning. I got
stuff to tell you about Jared. Come alone. I'll be watching
you."

Which is why, alone, at 8:20 A.M., I was parking along
the street by the park that led to the Rocks near the lake. It
had begun to rain again. Still light, but with the promise of
heavy in the low sky and the tumescent air. I didn't put on a
raincoat; I wanted quick access to my gun.

I was pretty sure Animal had nothing to tell me about
Jared. But the only way to know that was to show up and
ask him. My guess was he wanted to even things up a little,

which surprised me. Maybe he was spunkier than I gave him credit for. Or crazier.

Dowling was pretty quiet at this time on a rainy weekday morning. A car moved past the park now and then, carrying somebody to work somewhere. But to the extent that Dowling had a rush hour, it was over by now. Everybody else was sleeping in. The ground was soft from the wet summer, but the current rain was only a bit more than a mist. The park was empty as I squished through it. The trees that screened the Rocks deflected the light rain so that it seemed almost to have stopped. There was no wind. I could smell the lake. There was no sound. In the clearing where the Rocks started, lying on her back on the ground, was George. I stopped. She was dead. I'd seen too many bodies not to know. I jumped to my right and dropped flat on the ground behind the thick trunk of a big maple tree, and three shots tore through the low branches of the trees where I had been.

On my belly in the soaking leaf mold, I wriggled farther right, toward the big rock formation where the shots had come from, and nestled as flat into the muddy forest floor as I could. There was no sound. I took my gun off my hip and cocked it and waited. The rock formation he was behind was a good place to shoot from. I knew how it was supposed to go. I see George. I rush to her side and kneel beside her. He puts three slugs in me at close range and walks away. But it hadn't gone the way he thought it would, and now he was stuck. The rocks were isolated, and there was no way for him to leave them without exposing himself. I could wait. So could he. He did. I did. The silence of the woods once the gunshots had receded was smothering. It had begun to rain harder. I could feel the drops now, hitting my back as I lay in the mud. *Doesn't get much better than this.* I could outwait him. I could outwait Methuselah. I lay still. The silence pressed in on us. And the small rain down did rain. I smiled to myself. *Ah that my love were in my arms and I in my bed again.* Yes, I was a poetic devil, but at issue here, actually, was how well could I shoot. My gun had a two-inch barrel. And the cylinder held five rounds. I carried it because it was light, and because I had little need for distance shooting. But my guess was that he had a nine-millimeter with a longer barrel and maybe ten more rounds in the magazine. My gun would have to do. It's a poor work-man who blames his tools. The rain was pounding down now, and there was lightning in the distance followed apace by the roll of thunder. I took my Pirates hat off and put it over my gun hand to protect it from the rain. I didn't need to keep my powder dry. The thing would probably fire under water, but I didn't want it slippery wet in my hand. The lightning came again, and the thunder followed it more quickly. The rainwater plastered my hair to my skull, and the rain ran down over my forehead and into my eyes. I wiped it with the back of my wet hand. When I finished wiping, he was out from behind the rocks. No surprise. It was Animal, and he couldn't stand the waiting.

"Come out, motherfucker," he said. "Stand up and face me, tough guy."

He had a nine-millimeter and was waving it around.

"Come on, cocksucker. You think you so big, you man enough, you come out here and stand up to me."

He was probably fifty feet away.

"No sucker punching now," he shouted, "no cops around, motherfucker, just you and me."

It was hard to tell because he was yelling, but I thought he might be crying, too.

"Step out, you yellow cocksucker!" he said.

At fifty feet, I was pretty good with the little Smith and Wesson. The smart move was to drill him where he stood. I shook my hat off, which did no good, and put it on. I got up, screened by a low spread of white pine.

"One chance, Animal," I said. "Put the gun away."

He turned toward my voice. I moved left, and as fast as he could squeeze them off, he put five bullets through the white pine, tearing clumps of needles in their passage.

I stood sideways, aiming carefully, and squeezed off three shots at the middle of his mass, trying to group them around the lower end of his sternum. He yelled once, the way a weight lifter does when completing a lift, and stepped back. The gun dropped from his hands, and he fell sideways onto the wet earth. I stood for a moment, listening. Only the rain and the sporadic thunder. Nothing moved. There was no one else with him. I walked to him and looked at his gun. It was some sort of Italian nine-millimeter. I left it where it had landed and squatted beside him. He was dead. I moved over to George. She was dead, but less recently than Animal. I stood and looked down at both of them while I opened the cylinder and ejected the spent rounds and re-loaded. I put the gun back on my hip and snapped the holster strap.

He'd killed George for talking to me. And he wanted me to see that before he killed me for slapping him around. I thought I'd scared him enough. I hadn't. I guess he was spunkier than I'd thought. And the miscalculation had cost George her life and Animal his. Animal was bleeding from his chest. The rain was washing the blood pinkly away. When eventually I found out why Jared shot up his school, what would I have? The truth. Was that worth two bodies? The world had probably lost more for less. But they were alive, and now they weren't. Maybe the truth wasn't worth dying for. Or killing for. Maybe it never had been.

Too late now.

I looked at them some more. End of the line at, what, seventeen for her? He was maybe twenty-two. Then I stopped thinking and just looked at them as they lay in the mud, mindless of the rain.

After a while I went back to my car to call Cromwell.

42

DIBELLA SHOWED UP about forty-five minutes after Cromwell, and stood with us in the rain in the grove while the Dowling crime-scene specialist did what he could with the soaking crime scene. They both wore raincoats and hats. I didn't. I figured I had nothing to lose by getting rained on some more.

"Two more dead," Cromwell said.

I didn't say anything. Neither did DiBella.

"I don't like some know-it-fucking-all from the city coming out here and killing people in my town."

"Actually, that's person," I said. "Singular. I didn't kill the girl."

"And you don't think she'd be alive if you hadn't kept sticking your fucking snout into everything around here?"

"She might be," I said.

"On the other hand," DiBella said, "she's probably alive if whatsisname over there, Yang, doesn't shoot her in the fucking chest . . . several times."

Cromwell shrugged.

"How many times he shoot at you?" Cromwell said.

"Came pretty fast," I said. "I'd say eight."

"How much brass you find, Clyde?" Cromwell said to the crime-scene guy.

"Eight from the nine, three thirty-eights. Dead guy had six rounds left in his piece. One in the chamber, five in the magazine."

"Thirty-eights are mine," I said. "I reloaded."

"You thought there'd be more people?" Cromwell said.

"I always reload," I said.

From the periphery of my vision, I saw DiBella nod approval.

"So, if that's the case," Cromwell said, "then he probably shot her someplace else and brought her here."

"She's been dead awhile," Clyde said.

"How long," Cromwell said.

Clyde looked up at Cromwell squinting against the rain.

"Harry, I got no fucking clue. I do fingerprints and look for clues. I don't know shit about corpses."

"ME'll tell us," DiBella said.

"I want your gun," Cromwell said to me. "Ballistic comparison."

I nodded and took it out of its holster, unloaded it, and handed it to him.

"I'll need it back," I said.

"How do I know you didn't shoot her?" Cromwell said.

"ME'll tell you that she was shot with a nine," I said.

"You coulda had a nine."

"Sure, and before you came, I ate it and the brass."

"Maybe you didn't call us right away."

"C'mon, Harry," DiBella said to Cromwell. "You know he's legit. Besides, the crime scene matches his story."

"He could have arranged that," Cromwell said.

"Why, for crissake?" DiBella said. "You're just sulky 'cause there's another shooting in your town."

"I don't like it," Cromwell said.

"For crissake, Captain Healy vouched for him to me," DiBella said. "Shit happens."

"I don't like it when it happens in my town," Cromwell said.

"Nobody does," DiBella said. "But it's gotta happen someplace."

"We through here?" I said.

"What's your hurry?"

"My dog's home alone," I said. "She'll need a walk."

Cromwell looked puzzled.

"You need to borrow a piece until they return that one?" DiBella said.

"Got one in the car," I said.

"I hope it's locked up safe," Cromwell said.

"Gun safety is job one," I said.

Cromwell looked at me and then at DiBella and then at

the bodies on the ground and then at my stubby .38, which he was still holding.

"You can shoot," Cromwell said after a time. "I'll give you that."

I didn't say anything.

"Come by in a couple days," Cromwell said. "I'll see that you get the gun back."

"Am I free to go?" I said.

Cromwell stared at me for a minute.

"Yeah. Get some dry clothes. Come in tomorrow, give us a statement."

I nodded and turned toward the street. DiBella came, too.

"Where you going?" I said.

"You're unarmed," DiBella said. "I'm walking you to your car."

43

MY BACKUP GUN was a .357, which was heavy to wear, but I thought it worth the weight on this occasion. I was with Major Johnson and the bald guy with the prison tattoos who had shown such instant affection for me the first time we met. We were sitting on a bench at the edge of a hot top walkway in a playground in Roxbury. I was once again uniquely white.

There were black children playing on the swings and slides that the park commission had set up. There were black mothers and grandmothers, most of whom were younger than I was, watching the kids. There were some black teenagers smoking cigarettes and looking bad in gangsta-rap jeans and hats on sideways.

Past the play area, I could see Jose Yang and two of his people coming toward us. They sat across the hot top walkway from us on a bench just like ours. The management team of Los Diablos was as black as everyone else, except for Yang, whose skin tone was lighter, but far darker than mine.

The scary-looking teens watched us covertly. I was an aberration, and they would naturally have stared at me. But I was with two legitimate gangbangers, and I knew the kids were struggling to look just as dangerous, while desperately trying to do nothing that would annoy any of us.

Nobody spoke for a while. Jose Yang looked at me without expression.

"I killed your brother," I said.

Yang's face didn't move. No expression. The men on each side of him didn't do anything.

"Why?" Yang said.

"He tried to kill me," I said.

"Tell me."

I did. In outline form. Yang listened without any reaction.

"He shot the broad for talking to you," Yang said when I was finished.

I nodded.

"What it looks like," I said.

"And he tried to backshoot you?" Yang said.

I shrugged.

"He tried to shoot me from cover," I said.

"But at the end, he come out," Yang said.

"Yes."

"And you come out."

"Yes."

"Face-to-face," Yang said.

I nodded.

"He was looking at you when he died," Yang said.

"He was."

Yang stood suddenly and walked down the hot top walkway to the far end of the park and stood with his back to us, looking out at the tightly packed neighborhood around us. None of us on the benches did anything. After a time, Yang turned and walked back down the walkway and stood in front of me. He looked at me. I looked at him.

"He straight?" Yang said to Major.

"Yeah."

"You believe what he say?"

"Yeah."

"Why you come tell me?" Yang said to me.

"Didn't want to be looking behind me the rest of my life."

"He was my brother," Yang said.

I nodded.

"He a fucking fool, too," Yang said.

I nodded.

"Never knew how to act," Yang said.

"He stood up," I said. "At the end. He came at me straight-on."

Yang nodded.

"You got some big balls coming here like this," Yang said.

"Had to be done," I said.

"Like killing Luis," Yang said.

"Yeah," I said.

Yang nodded some more. He looked back at the corner

of the park where he had stood, as if there was something there only he could see.

"I got no problem with you," he said finally, still staring at the far corner of the park.

"Good," I said and stood.

Yang's gaze came slowly back from the corner and settled on me. He nodded.

"Sorry about your brother," I said.

Yang nodded again. He didn't speak. I had nothing else to say, so, with Major and his pal behind me, I turned and walked out of the park.

44

I SAT IN A BIG maple captain's chair in a small office in the Bethel County Courthouse and talked to Francis X. Cleary, the Bethel County Chief Prosecutor.

"I've heard a lot about you already," Cleary said.

He had longish silvery hair, which he combed straight back, and high color, and pale blue eyes that were very bright and never seemed to blink.

"So you are fully prepared to admire me," I said.

Cleary laughed.

"I'm maintaining a wait-and-see attitude," he said. "You convinced the Clark kid did it?"

"Yes," I said. "But I don't know why."

"And you care why," Clearly said.

"Yes."

"I don't," Cleary said. "We got his confession. His accomplice supports it."

Cleary spread his hands, palms up.

"Slam, bam," he said. "Thank you, ma'am."

He grinned at me happily.

"You had a shrink talk with him?"

"Naw. If the putz that's representing him goes for an insanity defense, I'll have somebody talk to him and say he's legally sane. If not, why waste the taxpayers' money."

"You've talked with him," I said.

"The kid? Sure. We've had several conversations with him. Always, of course, with his attorney present."

"Lawyer seems a little weak," I said.

"You want to do time," Cleary said. "Hire him. I wouldn't let him search a title for me."

"Off the record," I said. "Just you and me. What do you think?"

"About the kid?" Cleary said. "Oh, he did it. No doubt. But . . ."

"But?"

"But, there's something wrong with him," Cleary said.

I nodded.

"Besides the fact that he shot up his school," I said. "For no good reason."

"Besides that," Cleary said. "I been doing this a long time. I like it. I like putting them away and not letting them out. It's why I'm still doing it. I've talked to a lotta killers, a lotta whack jobs. But this kid . . . there's something missing, and I don't know what it is."

"Yeah," I said.

"I'm not in the business of helping people I'm prosecuting. I'm in the business of throwing away the key, and I'll do it with this kid, and never look back. But . . ."

"There's no sport in it," I said.

"Everybody wants to bury the kids, bury the crime, forget about it all. Parents want to bury him and move on. School. His fucking lawyer."

Cleary shook his head.

"It's barely an adversarial procedure," I said.

"At least the other kid's got Taglio."

"Good defense lawyer?"

"Decent," Cleary said. "I mean, he's got no case, but he's trying."

"If I can get somebody," I said, "will you let my shrink evaluate him?"

"So he can show up in court and say the poor lad's crazy, and I'll have to get my expert and put him on the stand and we'll have dueling shrinks?"

"No," I said. "The eval will be private, just with me. I won't make it available to anyone. Without your say-so."

Cleary looked at me, frowning.

"There's something wrong with him," I said.

Cleary kept frowning.

"Fish in a barrel?" I said.

Cleary grinned.

"I talked to Healy about you," he said.

I nodded.

"And I got a professional courtesy–type call from an attorney named Rita Fiore at Cone, Oakes and Beldon," he said. "In Boston. Used to be a prosecutor in Norfolk County."

"I know Rita," I said.

"Led me to believe that if I was nice to you, she'd come out some day and fuck my brains out."

"Ever met Rita?" I said.

Cleary grinned.

"Yes," he said. "That's why I'm being so nice."

"Can I send in my shrink?"

"Yeah. Call me when you're ready."

I stood up.

"Healy say nice things?" I said.

"Sort of," Cleary said. "But he made no mention of fucking."

"Isn't that good," I said.

45

IT WAS ALMOST MIDNIGHT when Susan called. She had been out to dinner.

"Magnolia Grill," she said, "in Durham, very nice."

"Anybody there I need to be jealous of?" I said.

"Lovenik," she said. "These are all highly educated mental-health professionals."

"Anyone there I need to be jealous of?"

"Several," she said. "Thank God."

"You still got it, kid."

"I hope so," she said.

We were quiet for a moment. Then we talked about how we wished we were together and what we would be doing if we were together.

"Is this phone sex?" I said at one point in the conversation.

"I think so," Susan said. "I hope the baby can't hear you."

"At this hour?" I said. "She's zonkered under the covers."

"Is she all right?"

"She's fine," I said. "She's been crime-busting with me."

"And brilliantly, too, I'll wager," Susan said.

"Think Rin Tin Tin," I said.

"Are you still on that school shooting?" Susan said.

"Yep."

"Is it hard going?"

"Yes."

"Did that boy really do it?" Susan said.

"I'm sure he did."

"So . . . ?"

"I want to know why," I said.

"There's always a *why*," Susan said.

"But there's not always somebody who knows what it is," I said.

"Not even the perpetrator sometimes," Susan said. "*Why* is hard."

"I need a shrink," I said.

"I've told you that for years," she said.

"I have you," I said. "But you're not here."

"We both regret that," Susan said.

"I want somebody to evaluate the kid for me," I said.

Susan was quiet for a moment. Under the covers, Pearl made a soft lip-smacking noise, and shifted so that her head stuck out. The process took most of the covers from me.

"There's a man named Dix," Susan said. "He's in private practice, works a lot with cops."

"Alcohol and depression," I said.

"Of course," Susan said. "He also consults forensically. I don't know from here how to get him. But he's probably in the book. Or you can find him through the Boston Psychiatric Institute."

"He a psychiatrist?"

"Yes."

"He got a first name?"

"Of course, but I don't know it. I met him last year during a seminar at Brandeis. He calls himself Dix. He's quite handsome."

"Handsomer than anyone?" I said.

"Sure," Susan said.

I waited. She didn't say anything. I waited some more. Then she said, "Except, of course, you, Hunko."

"Thank you," I said.

46

I WAS DRIVING a dark green Mustang this year, with a tan top, which, when I drove it with the top down, wearing my Oakley shades, did in fact suggest the designation *Hunko*. While Susan was away and I had Pearl, I parked the Mustang in Susan's driveway and used Susan's white Explorer so that Pearl would have sufficient room to jump around and annoy me.

But now I was at the last desperate fallback position, where, under Spenser's Rule #113, you find someone to follow, and follow them. So I rented a tannish-grayish Toyota Camry sedan, which looked like 40 percent of the other cars on the road, and, with Pearl looking a little disgruntled in the backseat, I parked outside Channing Hospital and watched for Beth Ann Blair.

Like everyone else who had come and gone while I sat there, she paid me no heed as she came down the front walk of the hospital and turned left toward the parking lot. The Toyota was working. It was so effective that I could still wear my Oakleys and be overlooked. I admired her stride as she went into the lot. Susan had explained to me that the amount of hip sway was usually dependent on the kinds of shoes you were wearing, but I was pretty sure that in Beth Ann's case, it also suggested a kind of pelvic awareness that might be prideful.

She had one of those little boxy Audi sports cars that reminded me of German sports cars from the 1930s. It was silver. She turned left out of the parking lot, and I fell in a ways behind and followed. Tailing somebody in the country is easy in the sense that you won't lose them, but hard in the sense that you're easy to spot. Beth Ann wasn't expecting to be followed, which was an advantage. My car was not noticeable. And, of course, city or country, it helped that I could track better than Natty Bumppo.

She stopped at the village market. I lingered up the street. She came out with a bag of something and got back in her car. Off we went. She stopped for gasoline on Route 20. I lingered around a turn. She pumped it herself, which was impressive. Susan would run out of gas and leave the car and walk home before she'd use a self-service pump. Then, with a full tank, she got back in the car, started up, and drove past me, and I followed. We got all the way to Framingham before she turned off into the parking lot of a large brick condominium complex that overlooked a lake. She parked and got out with her groceries and went in.

Pearl and I sat. Beth Ann didn't come out. After a time, I took Pearl out for a short, necessary stroll to a small patch of grass under a single tree. I could still see the door of Beth Ann's building while Pearl occupied herself. Then we got back in the car. And sat. It got dark. I broke out a bag of sandwiches, which I had hidden in the trunk to keep Pearl from ravaging them, and a couple of bottles of spring water. I ate a ham and cheese on light rye, and gave Pearl a roast beef on whole wheat. She finished first. There were two sandwiches left. I put them back in the trunk. Back in the car, I drank some water and gave some to Pearl. Drinking from the bottle, she slobbered a lot onto the backseat but managed to swallow enough to alleviate thirst and prevent dehydration.

At about 9:30, I gave it up. Beth Ann had made no further appearance. She might slip out later and perform some criminal act, but it was more likely that she was in bed in her jammies, reading *Civilization and Its Discontents*, and I was tired. Pearl and I gave it up and went home.

47

DIX HAD A PERFECTLY bald head, and big square hands, and a strong neck. I would not have called him handsome myself, but maybe I was just holding him unfairly to the Hunko standard. He looked like he had just shaved before I came in. His head glistened. His nails were manicured. His white shirt gleamed. He had on a blue blazer with bright brass buttons, and the crease in his gray slacks looked like it would cut paper.

"Captain Healy called me about you," Dix said.

"And you still agreed to see me," I said.

Dix smiled and didn't answer. Shrinks don't banter.

"You recall the school shoot-up in Dowling," I said.

"Yes."

"I would like you to talk to one of the participants, kid named Jared Clark."

Dix nodded. He sat erect in his chair, elbows resting on the arms, thick fingers laced across his flat stomach. Eyes resting steadily on my face. Entirely motionless. I wondered what Susan was like in session.

"There's something wrong with him," I said. "I want to know what."

"Are you asking me to judge him legally sane or insane?" Dix said.

"No."

"Does he wish to talk with me?"

"I doubt it."

"Do you have any predisposed theory on what might be wrong?"

"No. He's . . . He's off. . . . All the pieces don't quite fit."

"Do you want a diagnosis on the basis of a single interview?"

"Up to you," I said. "You give me a diagnosis as soon as you think you have one."

"Unless I have him willingly for a considerable time, it's more likely to be a guess."

"But an informed one," I said. "It's not something that you'll have to swear to under oath. I'm just looking for help."

"Do you think he is innocent?"

"No. I think he did it."

Dix raised his eyebrows and looked his question at me.

"His grandmother and I want to know why," I said. "Maybe if we know, there'll be a way to mitigate his sentence."

"An apostle of the possible," Dix said.

"Yes."

"You're with Susan Silverman," Dix said.

"Yes."

"So you have some understanding of our business."

"Yes."

"What is his attorney's position on this?" Dix said.

"His attorney," I said, "like everyone else, as far as I can see, except his grandmother and me, including the kid, wants him to disappear quickly into the prison system and never reappear."

"Would his attorney object?" Dix said.

"He might," I said.

"Would access be a problem?"

I shook my head.

"The Bethel County DA will get us in," I said.

Dix raised his eyebrows.

"Really?" he said.

"My deal with Cleary is that he lets us in, and anything we learn will be between us, and not be used in court."

Dix was silent for a time. Entirely motionless, looking at me.

"What if I determine that he's legally insane and unfit to stand trial."

"Cleary's a decent guy," I said. "We tell him what we learn. If he's convinced, he'll have his own people take a look. He wants to win the case, and he's under a lot of pressure to do so, but he doesn't want to put a seventeen-year-old kid away for life if there's, ah, mitigation."

Dix was silent some more.

"Why not ask Dr. Silverman," Dix said.

"She's in North Carolina," I said.

"Ah, the conference at Duke," Dix said.

I nodded.

"I've met her several times," Dix said. "Very impressive woman."

"Impresses the hell out of me," I said.

Dix smiled. A breakthrough!

"You have said *we* in talking about the interview," Dix said. "If I do this, I'll talk to the boy alone."

"I'll wait outside the room," I said.

Dix nodded.

"Okay," he said. "I can do this. Who will be paying the charges?"

"I will."

"Then you'll need to know my fee."

"I don't," I said. "But I think it's part of your deal to tell me."

"It is," Dix said.

And he told me.

48

I WAS GETTING pretty bored following Beth Ann Blair around. Pearl seemed to mind less. On the other hand, if she weren't sleeping in the backseat of the Camry, she would have been sleeping on the couch in my office, or the bed in my home. The arc of the experience was fairly tight. It was Friday night. Pearl and I had just finished visiting the patch of grass under the single tree, and were sharing a bottle of water in the car, when Royce Garner, the president of the Dowling School, his very self, pulled up in a Buick sedan and parked near the front door and got out and went in carrying a small suitcase.

"Ho, ho!" I said to Pearl.

We sat that night until 1:30 A.M. without any reappearance by Garner. And at 9:12 the next morning when I got there, with a large coffee, the Buick was still where it had been.

"Highly suspicious," I said.

But Pearl wasn't with me. She was with Susan's dog runner this morning, in the woods, somewhere west of Cambridge. Probably wasn't much sillier talking to myself than it would have been talking to a dog. The morning crept past. Lunchtime came and crept on by. Fortunately, when I bought the coffee, I'd also purchased half a dozen doughnuts for just such an emergency. I ate a couple. At about three-thirty in the afternoon, Garner came out alone and got in his car and drove away. I followed him uneventfully to a comfortable-looking white colonial house next to the Dowling School. He parked in the driveway, took out his small suitcase, and walked to the front door. Someone opened it, I couldn't see who, and Garner went in.

My doughnuts were gone. I knew what I knew, and there was no reason to keep reknowing it. The next step was to figure out what to do about what I knew. So I went home.

Actually, I went to Susan's house. The dog runner had left Pearl there, so I went and let Pearl out and fed her and sat at the counter in Susan's silent, immaculate kitchen and drank some Johnnie Walker Blue with a lot of ice and soda.

After she finished eating, Pearl snuffled rapidly through every room in the house once more to make absolutely sure Susan was in fact not there. Then Pearl came back in the kitchen and settled onto the couch provided for her.

"I know," I said. "If I had a better nose, that's what I would have done, too."

Pearl raised her head and wagged her tail at me from the couch.

"She'll be back," I said. "Couple of weeks."

Pearl settled onto the couch and put her head on her paws and watched me, moving her eyes only, in case I should suddenly try to eat something. I drank some scotch. Susan's place sounded like an empty house, the hush of the air-conditioning, the barely audible hum of the refrigerator, the hint of street sound. Occasionally, the creak of floor joists settling half a millimeter. I could smell her perfume. The house was rich with colors: gold and green and burgundy and brown and tan and cream. There were rugs and drapes and throws, and paintings and lamps and trays, and stuff that had no other function than to be stunning.

My drink was gone. I went to the refrigerator and got more ice. There were a couple of Lean Cuisines in the freezer. In the main part of the refrigerator, there was half a bottle of Kendall-Jackson Riesling, and a navel orange. There was no cork in the half-empty bottle; it was covered with a small Baggie fastened with a blue elastic band. I smiled. Everything spoke of her. I added scotch and some soda to my drink and sat back at the counter. Around the kitchen were pictures of me and Susan and Pearl. There were seven pictures of Pearl. Three of me and Susan. If I weren't such a Hunko, it might have given me pause. The house was her: elegant, flamboyant, beautiful. *A thing worth doing*, Susan always said, *was worth overdoing*. I stood and took my drink and walked into the living room. Everything you could sit on in there had so many pillows on it that you'd have to move them to make room for your tush. There were more pictures of Pearl and me. Same ratio. There was a picture of her mother and father, dark-haired and European-looking, though I knew her father ran a drugstore in Swampscott. There were pictures of Susan with people I didn't know. There was no sign of her ex-husband.

I went into the bedroom. The Spenser/Pearl ratio improved. There was one large picture, of me with Pearl beside me. The picture, in a big, clear acrylic frame, sat on her night table. There were no other pictures. There were so many decorative pillows on the bed that you couldn't sit on it, either, let alone sleep. I looked at the bed for a time and smelled her perfume more insistently. I felt my stomach tighten.

"Couple of weeks," I said. "Couple of weeks."

I went to the kitchen for a refill. Pearl had lost all interest in me, and was asleep now on her couch. I sat back on my stool at the counter and felt the scotch move through me happily.

So, Beth Ann and Royce were spending nights together. So what? What Beth Ann was telling me about Jared didn't jibe with what everyone else was telling me about Jared. So what?

I wondered if the romance with Garner was surreptitious. I wondered if Garner were married. Someone had greeted him at the door when he went home. I wondered what it all had to do with Jared, if anything. I sipped my scotch. Susan's home was built in the nineteenth century. It had high ceilings and wide hallways. Her office was downstairs. Her self was everywhere. If I weren't so autonomous and self-reliant, I would have missed her like a bastard.

"Being a seasoned investigator," I said to Pearl, "I have found that when there's stuff you don't know in a case, it's best to find it out."

Pearl was on her back, her head lolled off the couch, and she looked at me upside down. I finished my drink.

"Tomorrow," I said.

I got up and went to Susan's bedroom and cleared space among the pillows and went to bed. Pearl joined me later in the night.

49

I HAD RETURNED my Camry. Pearl was off to the woods with the woman Susan insisted on calling Pearl's personal trainer. I sat in my office with coffee, going through the scrapbook of press clippings that Lily Ellsworth had given me when I first met her. I thought I remembered something, and I was right. There was a picture of Royce Garner with Mrs. Garner beside him, talking to a group of parents during the crisis. She looked like an answer to the question *Why does Mr. Garner fool around?* Of course, she might be a wonderful human being. But unless the camera lied flagrantly, no one would mistake her for pretty.

So it was surreptitious. Garner was cheating on his wife with Beth Ann. Why Beth Ann would wish to cheat on anyone with Royce Garner was imponderable. So I didn't ponder it. Instead, I pondered what I could do with what I had learned. After a while, I decided on B&E, with blackmail a fallback position, and took my coffee, got my gym bag of tools, went to my car, and headed out to Beth Ann's condo to implement my plan.

It was mid-morning when I got there. The sun was bright. The weather was cool. The condo parking lot was half empty. A guy in a white sleeveless undershirt was rolling a big blue trash barrel across the lot. He set it down at the far edge of the lot, beside another one, and turned and went back around the building. After he disappeared, I drove around behind the building and down a slight grade. At the basement level, a big door stood open. The guy in the undershirt came out with another big blue barrel. He had a wreath tattooed around the biceps of his left arm. I parked in a guest overflow slot near the basement door. The guy in the undershirt ignored me, and when he was out of sight, I left my car, took my small gym bag with me, and walked into the basement. I was in an open area where there were at least ten more of the big blue barrels. Ahead of me was a corridor. I went down it. There was a boiler room to the left, and at the far end, two elevators. I got in one. I punched the button for the lobby and went up.

In the lobby, I opened the front door of the building. I used my tool bag to keep it from closing, went out, found Beth Ann's name on the directory. 417. I went back in, picked up my gym bag, and took the elevator to the fourth floor. Number 417 was at the far end of the corridor, on the left, which probably meant Beth Ann paid less for it and didn't get to look at the lake. I put my gym bag down and knocked. No answer. Breaking into a place isn't very hard if you don't mind people knowing you were there. Tossing a place and having no one know it was a little trickier. I didn't care if Beth Ann knew someone had burgled her. So with a lender pry bar and a little force, I was in quite quietly in about two minutes. The jamb was splintered a bit and the door wouldn't latch closed anymore. But no one dashed into the corridor and yelled "Stop, thief!" I closed it and put my gym bag down to keep it from swinging open, and turned my attention to the apartment.

Beth Ann was not an obsessive housekeeper. The breakfast dishes were still on the coffee table. There was lingerie on the floor of the bathroom and a bathrobe tossed across the sofa in the living room. Two empty wine bottles stood on the sideboard, and a cutting board with vestiges of cheese and stale bread sat beside them. In an alcove off the living room, behind the kitchen, was home-office space with a desk and a laptop computer and a file cabinet. The computer was a Mac, which meant I had a feeble grasp of how it worked. I turned it on, and when it lit up, I clicked on the mail icon and read her e-mail. Most of it was innocuous. There were several embarrassing e-mails from someone named roygar, whom I assumed to be Garner. But nothing that added to my sum of useful knowledge. Nothing in the computer referred to Jared.

I moved to the file cabinet and spent more than two hours going through professional mail outgoing, professional mail incoming, bills tendered, bills paid, credit-card statements, a file of clippings about the school shooting in Dowling, a file of love letters from Garner that would have made a buzzard feel queasy, and about five years' worth of at-a-glance appointment calendars, none of which told me anything more than she had a busy life. I took the love letters and put them in my gym bag.

I moved to the desk. It had a checkbook and bank statements in the center drawer. They indicated that she spent a lot of money, but nothing else. I spent an hour on the desk. If I had known what I was looking for, it would have gone faster. I could eliminate places where what I wanted wouldn't go. But since I didn't know what I was looking for, I had to look everywhere. I checked under the throw rug in the bedroom, and under the bed, and between the mattress and box spring, and in the towels folded in the closet, and the pockets of coats. I sifted through sweaters and underwear and socks. I looked in the toes of her shoes. I checked behind paintings and mirrors, under couch cushions, behind chairs. In the bathroom, I checked the toilet tank. In the kitchen, I looked into cereal boxes and sugar canisters. I checked in the oven and under the sink. I looked in the refrigerator, in the vegetable keeper, behind bottles of Perrier. I opened the freezer and found something. Under a package of frozen chicken thighs, in a plastic freezer-storage bag with a tightly sealed top, was a six-by-nine brown envelope. In the envelope were pictures of Jared Clark and Beth Ann Blair. Both were naked.

I said, "Bingo."

My voice was loud in the empty apartment.

There were five pictures; none showed them having sex, and all showed them in affectionate full-frontal nudity. Probably taken with a timer, which would be more difficult in mid–sexual congress.

She couldn't get rid of them. There was absolutely

nothing else in the apartment that even hinted of any connection to Jared Clark. But whatever made a grown woman take up with an early-adolescent boy made her, in the face of all wisdom, keep these unforgiving mementos in deep concealment.

I closed the freezer, put the pictures in my gym bag along with my burglar tools, and went out of the apartment. When she came home and found she'd been broken into, she'd go straight to the freezer. In five minutes, she'd know the pictures were gone. She would be sick with worry and fear and maybe shame. *Good!* I took the elevator down to the lobby. There was no one in the lobby. I went out the front door and walked around the building to where I'd parked my car. The basement door was closed now. I started the car and drove out through the parking lot. All the blue barrels were lined up in an orderly row, waiting for the trash truck. The sun was in the western sky. I looked at my watch; it was after four. I pulled out onto the highway and drove toward Cambridge to retrieve Pearl.

50

I MET DIX in the parking lot of the Bethel County Jail.

"I thought you probably should know before you talk to Jared," I said. "There was a sexual relationship between him and Beth Ann Blair, the school shrink."

"You know this how?"

"I have photographs."

"Which you got how?"

"By breaking into Dr. Blair's condo," I said.

"Does the DA know this?" Dix said.

"No one knows it but you and me and, I assume, Dr. Blair."

Dix nodded. "Okay," he said.

We went into the jail. Cleary was waiting for us at the interview room. I introduced them.

"Jared know who I am?" Dix said.

"He's been told you are a psychiatrist come at our behest to interview him," Cleary said.

"Did you tell him he had to talk with me?"

"I told him he had to show up. Talking was up to him."

"Is there any way you can overhear us?" Dix said.

"Sure," Cleary said.

"No," Dix said.

"No?"

"It will be private between the boy and me," Dix said.

Cleary didn't like Dix's manner.

"Why?" Cleary said.

"I need to be able to assure him that what he says is between me and him."

"You could lie a little," Cleary said.

"No," Dix said. "I couldn't."

"So what if I don't agree?" Cleary said.

"I won't do it unless you agree."

"So why do I care if you do or don't?" Cleary looked at me. "I'm doing him the favor."

"Private or not?" Dix said.

"Christ, you are a real hard-on," Cleary said. "Aren't you."

"Glad you noticed," Dix said. "Private or no?"

"Private," Cleary said.

"Thanks," Dix said and opened the door to the interview room and went in. The door closed behind him.

"Embarrassing," I said to Cleary, "the way he sucked up to you."

"I'm just the people's attorney," Cleary said.

"That's what filled him with awe," I said.

"Probably," Cleary said. "You want some coffee?"

"The coffee here any good?" I said.

"Unspeakable," Cleary said.

"I'll have some," I said.

The coffee was in fact brutal, but I drank it manfully.

"You're giving us a lot of slack," I said to Cleary.

He shrugged and sipped his coffee and made a face.

"I got a conviction," he said. "I can play it a little loose."

"And you want to know more than you do," I said.

He shrugged again. "I'd like things to make sense," he said, "if they can."

"We both know they often don't," I said.

"Doesn't mean there's no sense to be made," Cleary said.

I nodded. We drank our coffee. Cleary put down his cup, as if he was relieved to have finished it. He stood.

"I got work to do," he said.

"Thank you," I said, "for setting this up."

"Dix finds out anything interesting," Cleary said, "you know where I am."

"I do," I said.

After Cleary left, I sat alone in the ugly room for two and a half more hours, and used the time to not drink any more coffee. It was nearly one o'clock in the afternoon when Dix came out of the interview room.

51

THE RANGE of lunch choices around the Bethel County Jail was narrow. We left Dix's car in the jail lot and I drove us to the village market in Dowling, where I had eaten pie with DiBella the first time I met him. We took a little table inside and ordered a couple of sandwiches. Dix ordered coffee with his. I had a glass of milk to cleanse my palate. A nearly intact pie sat promisingly under a glass dome on the counter.

"Your boy is retarded," Dix said.

"That's a fact or an informed guess?"

"Like most other branches of medicine, psychiatry is both an art and a science. Most of our conclusions tend to be informed guesses."

"His grades are good. He was on course to graduate. He

seemed able to plan a shootout at his school. How retarded can he be?"

"Mildly," Dix said.

"What does that mean?"

"It means mildly. We can test him at length and come up with a number, but for our purposes, *mildly retarded* will work."

"So how come no one seems to have noticed it?" I said.

"No one else was looking for it. You knew that there was something wrong with him."

"Yes," I said. "Actually, his parents probably noticed it, too."

"And didn't want to see it."

"Yeah. It's probably why his grandmother was so protective. He always been retarded?"

"I'd need a lot more time to answer that, and I'm not sure it would be time well spent. My guess is that he's functionally retarded."

"Meaning?"

"Meaning he has not learned to function at the level one would have anticipated."

"So he may not have been born retarded."

"He may not. There are a number of possible explanations. But the fact remains that he is now at least mildly impaired."

"Could he live a, I don't know what to call it, normal life?"

"With help," Dix said, "probably."

"He say anything about his relationship with Beth Ann Blair?"

"I didn't ask. He didn't tell," Dix said. "I was not there to question him about the crime."

"You think it had something to do with the crime?"

"In fact, of course, I don't know," Dix said. "A relationship which had proceeded to nudity, between a fully sexual adult woman and a barely pubescent retarded boy, would be a very powerful event in the boy's life. And if that boy stands accused of mass murder . . ."

Our sandwiches sat waiting and waiting on their paper plates on the counter. I stood up and got them and set them on the table. Dix had ham on light rye. I had tongue on light rye. I got a second glass of milk for me and another coffee for Dix.

"Is he retarded enough that we could use it in some sort of impairment defense?"

"I need more information. I'd want to know what role the woman played in his behavior." Dix took in a long, slow breath through his nose and let it out. "But basically, I doubt it. I doubt that his mental retardation prevented him from understanding the illegality of his actions any more than, if you are an accurate reporter, and I suspect that you are, it prevented him from some rather lengthy and careful preparation for his crime."

I nodded.

"If, on the other hand, you could establish some sort of obsessive circumstance with Dr. Blair . . ."

"Whatever the circumstance," I said, "it couldn't have been good."

Dix shrugged.

"You think it could be okay?" I said.

"I have been doing what I do," Dix said, "for a long time. I have found almost nothing that people do which is always good or always bad. How about you?"

I nodded.

"But for a kid like that," I said, "to suddenly start murdering people at random. Isn't the crime itself proof that the criminal is crazy?"

Dix smiled at me.

"You know and I know that if you start asking that question too insistently, you find yourself on a slippery, slippery slope. If doing the crime is proof of insanity, and sanity is a defense against conviction, then the crime is its exculpation, and no one is responsible for anything."

"And ten thousand years of what might optimistically be called civilization," I said, "goes right down the slope, too."

"On the other hand, if Dr. Blair was involved, and he was obsessed, and you have a good lawyer available . . ."

"Would you examine him further?" I said.

"As needed," Dix said.

"Would you testify?"

"I would testify to what I believed to be the truth," Dix said.

"Or as close as we can get to it," I said.

"One can get pretty close," Dix said, "if one keeps at it."

"Keeping at it is one of my best things," I said.

"Apparently," Dix said.

When we finished our sandwiches, we had some pie. It was blueberry this time. And none the worse for being so.

52

"GARNER'S HUMPING the school shrink?" DiBella said.

We were sitting in DiBella's car, parked on the main street in Dowling, a block from the Coffee Nut.

"Wouldn't you?" I said.

"Yeah, sure, but why would she?"

"Excellent question." I said. "When there are studs like you and me around."

"I'm not so sure about you," DiBella said.

"Actually, I included you," I said, "to be kind."

DiBella nodded. "Now we got that out of the way," he said. "And the school shrink was humping the Clark kid?"

"She was at least taking her picture naked with him."

"You wouldn't have it on you," DiBella said.

"Degenerate," I said.

"Sure, like you haven't studied it," DiBella said.

"Of course I have," I said. "It's evidence."

"Of what?" DiBella said. "Blair's snatch?"

"Well," I said. "Yes."

"Maybe I should see what I can dig up on both of them," DiBella said. "Garner and Blair."

"I thought you had this case closed already, and were just humoring me," I said.

"I'm in the habit," DiBella said. "I may as well humor you some more."

"Hard to believe it wouldn't have something to do with the shooting," I said.

"Pretty big set of coincidences," DiBella said.

"I don't know where it takes us," I said.

"That's why it's called investigation," DiBella said. "We see where it takes us."

From the backseat of DiBella's car, Pearl barked at a tan mongrel that went by on the other end of the leash from a middle-aged woman in cropped pants and a straw sun hat.

"Did you know," DiBella said, "that I'm not allowed to transport animals in my car?"

"Yes," I said. "I did know that."

DiBella nodded. I asked Pearl to stop barking. Which she did.

"I'll keep an eye on Blair and Garner," I said. "Maybe you could check out their history a little."

"Of course," DiBella said. "I have the vast resources of the criminal justice system at my fingertips. At your fucking service."

"Thanks."

"Your shrink says the kid is retarded?" DiBella said.

"Uh-huh."

"Cleary know that?" DiBella said.

"Uh-huh."

"What's he say?"

"Nothing," I said.

"Cleary says that a lot," DiBella said. "Which one you going to tail?"

"I'll probably take turns," I said. "And maybe I'll have a talk with Mrs. Garner."

"Gonna rat him out?" DiBella said.

"No. I'll make up some excuse," I said. "But it might energize him a little if he knows I talked with her."

"The way she's probably energized already," DiBella said, "knowing somebody's got her husband's number."

"And if they're energized together, maybe they'll do something."

"Like what," DiBella said.

"No idea," I said, "but maybe I'll catch them doing it."

53

MRS. GARNER was everything her picture in the paper had led me to believe she would be: squat, grim, and graceless. She let me into the house sullenly, and pointed me into a chair in the living room.

"Sorry to bother you," I said.

"But you're doing it anyway," she said.

"I am," I said cheerily.

The living room was shabby. The couch was a dark oak frame covered with worn green plush. It sagged in spots where too many people had sat too heavily for too long. I sat in a straight-back rush-bottom chair on which the original rush had been replaced by an inexpensive plastic substitute. She wore a grayish housedress with a tiny floral print on it. Her sneakers were old and white and low, with the toe cut away in one of them to relieve pressure on a bunion. Her gray hair was in a tight perm. There was a fireplace, which appeared to burn a gas log. On the wall above it was a much too big portrait of Garner in academic robes, wearing a mortarboard and holding a rolled-up scroll of some kind.

"What do you want?" Mrs. Garner said.

I gave her a wide, warm, and compelling smile. "I'm just trying to tie up loose ends of the terrible shooting at the school," I said.

She showed no reaction. Maybe she hadn't noticed my smile. I laid the smile on her again. Women have been known to show me their undergarments when I give them that smile. Thankfully, Mrs. Garner did not. She was sitting in a large padded rocker. On the table beside her was a decanter of something, maybe port. She was drinking some of it from a small wineglass. She didn't offer me any. I didn't mind. Port is never my first choice, and especially so on the morning side of lunch.

"Did you know either of the boys?" I said.

"No."

"Do you know many of the students at the school?"

"No."

She emptied her glass and poured herself some more. It smelled like port.

"How about faculty?"

"I have little to do with Royce's school," she said.

"Did you know any of the people killed?"

"Not really."

"Do you know Dr. Blair, the school psychologist?"

"The one who looks like a whore?"

I smiled dazzlingly before I remembered that it didn't seem to be working here.

"Eye of the beholder," I said.

"I don't know her, anyway," Mrs. Garner said. "I saw her once, someplace."

"Do you have children, Mrs. Garner?"

"No."

"Do you remember where you saw Beth Ann Blair?"

"No."

I was really running on all cylinders. Mr. Interrogation!

"Everything all right in your marriage?" I said.

"None of your business," she said.

I nodded. "Gee," I said. "I hadn't thought of it that way."

She said nothing.

"Well," I said. "I won't bother you anymore."

"Good."

I stood.

"Give my best to your husband," I said.

She didn't answer. I tried the smile once more. It was too late. But I couldn't believe it wasn't working.

"Enjoy your day," I said.

At last she decided to heed my advice. As I started for the front door, she poured herself more port.

54

I HAD FINISHED the morning paper and was cutting out today's episode of "Arlo and Janis" to save for Susan when the Clark family, including Lily Ellsworth and minus Jared, came into my office with their lawyer, Richard Leeland. Pearl raised her head and growled at them from her place on the couch. I shushed her as I stood.

"We need to talk," Leeland said.

"Sure," I said and came around my desk and organized the chairs. Pearl settled back but kept her eyes open, alert for a false move. Nobody made one. Everyone sat.

"My daughter," Lily Ellsworth said after a moment. "And my son-in-law, and this lawyer want me to fire you."

"Eek," I said.

Leeland leaned forward and started to speak.

"The boy is . . ."

Lily Ellsworth turned her head and looked at him.

"I am neither senile nor a dolt," she said. "I am able to talk for myself."

"Of course, Mrs. Ellsworth . . ."

She gestured for him to be quiet and looked back at me.

"You feel that Jared is retarded," she said.

"Functionally retarded," I said. "Yes."

"You have had him examined by a competent psychiatrist," she said.

"Yes."

"Without permission," Leeland said.

"Shut up!" Lily said without looking at him.

Leeland glanced at Ron and Dot and shook his head slightly, exhaled a long, suffering breath, and was quiet.

"They don't believe you," Lily said.

"Doesn't mean it's not so," I said.

"You believe it is so."

"Yes."

"They say even if it is so, he'll still have to go to jail."

"Yes."

"He did it," she said.

"Yes."

Lily was silent. She knew. She probably always knew but told herself it wasn't so.

"He's where he should be," Dot Clark said softly.

Lily waved at her to be quiet.

"Please, Dorothy," she said. "I'm trying to think what is best for my grandson."

Dot squealed as if someone had jabbed her with a sharp instrument. Lily flinched at the sound.

"Grandson?" Dot said. "Grandson? He's my fucking son, Mother. He's my only goddamned child. He killed a bunch of people. Maybe he's retarded, maybe he's crazy, but he did what he did. He's where he belongs."

"I'm trying to do what's best for him," Lily said.

Her voice was surprisingly quiet.

"Do what's best for me," Dorothy said. "Do you know what this has been like for me? For us? We enter a room and there's an uncomfortable pause. People pretend not to see me in the market."

"Dorothy," Lily said.

"Shut up," Dorothy said. "How does this shrink know? How can he spend three hours with him and say our son is retarded, and we've lived with him all his life and saw no sign? Who the hell does he think he is? How nice it will be for us if people now think we harbored this murderous retard all his life and never did anything about it."

"Dot," her husband said to her.

She turned toward him in her chair and screamed at him.

"You shut up, too. What if he got out? Do you want to live the rest of your life worried what he's going to do next, watching him all the time? Terrified every time he goes out? Fearful for yourself even when he's home? He's where he should be. Can't you all see that? Can't you fucking all see that? He's gone already. We've lost him already. Lost him, lost him, lost him . . ."

She started to cry. It was a bad sound—loud, blubbering, graceless, agonized, and very unpleasant to hear. Her husband put a hand on her shoulder. She pushed it away. She wanted to be alone in her misery.

"Even if his mental situation is confirmed," Leeland said, "they won't let him go."

I nodded.

Lily Ellsworth's eyes looked a little moist. But her voice was steady.

"Is that true?" she said.

"There are some things I still haven't fully figured out yet," I said. "Some things that might explain why, and might be mitigating."

"If you do, and they are," Lily said, "what is the best that Jared can hope for?"

"He's not an attorney," Leeland said.

"I sometimes wonder if you are," she said. "I trust him. What can you get him, best-case scenario?"

"An easier room in hell," I said.

"Oh, God," Dot said, still crying.

Her mother sat erect. Her face seemed gray; the skin seemed tightly stretched.

"And you believe he did what they accuse him of," she said.

"What he confessed to," Ron said.

She ignored him. She looked at me, waiting.

"Yes, ma'am," I said.

She turned toward her daughter and rested her hand on Dot's shoulder. Dot let it stay there.

"I am a forceful woman," Lily said, "and I am rich. And I have never seen any reason why I shouldn't get what I want."

Dot nodded faintly.

"But I love you," Lily said. Her voice was a little shaky.

"Mama," Dot said.

Dot leaned out of her chair, put her head against Lily's chest. Lily put her arms around her and patted her softly on the back. She looked past her daughter's head at me.

"It is over, Mr. Spenser. Send me your final bill. . . . I thank you for your effort."

"Yes, ma'am," I said.

Then Lily began to cry, and she and her daughter cried softly together with their arms around each other. It was not at all unpleasant to hear.

55

"So it's over," Cleary said to me.

I sat with him and Sergeant DiBella in Cleary's office at the courthouse.

"I still want to know the deal with Beth Ann Blair and Royce Garner," I said.

"Even though no one's paying you," DiBella said. "And the lady was paying you wants you to stop."

"Yuh," I said. "That's about right."

"You're a pushy bastard," Cleary said. "I suspect you'll find that out in a while."

"I suspect that, too," I said.

"So, what will you do with it?"

"If it had nothing to do with the school shootup," I said, "I'll forget about it. I don't care who bangs whom."

"Whom?" DiBella said.

"Whom," I said.

"I'll be surprised if that's what you find out," Cleary said.

"Me, too."

"So if you find out it's germane?" Cleary said.

"Jesus Christ," DiBella said. "Germane?"

"Try to learn from us," I said to DiBella.

DiBella grinned.

"What'll you do?" Cleary said.

"We'll talk," I said.

DiBella took a small notebook from his inside pocket and opened it.

"Beth Ann Blair," he said, looking at the notebook, "has been a school shrink in Santa Cruz, California; Louisville, Kentucky; Vero Beach, Florida; and Belfast, Maine. All private schools, all coed."

"Moves around a lot," I said.

"Nothing suspicious anywhere," DiBella said. "She stays a couple years at a school, moves on."

"Be interesting to talk to the students who were there when she was."

"For crisssake, Spenser," DiBella said. "I got no budget for this. We got no case here. Kid confessed. You even agree he did it."

"She's a child molester," I said.

"There's that," Cleary said. "And you say you've got the photo to prove it. But if you open that up, then don't you open up the whole Jared Clark thing?"

"That's why we're just three pals chewing the fat," I said.

"Until you find out whom this is all germane to," Di-Bella said.

"Nice," I said.

"I'm a fast learner," DiBella said.

"I got no problem letting you roam," Cleary said. "But I'm the chief prosecutor in Bethel County, and I take the job seriously."

"I heard that," I said.

"So, it's cool, as long as your interests and mine coincide," Cleary said. "But as soon as I decide they don't the leash is going to get a lot shorter."

"I sort of guessed that," I said.

"So you want to keep shaking this tree for a while on your own, for free, be my guest. Be kind of interesting to see if something falls out."

"It will be," I said.

"And in case you feel like getting cute, remember I can be a lot more unpleasant than I am now," Cleary said.

"Wow!" I said.

56

SOMETHING FELL from the tree quite promptly. I was in my office bright and early the next day, studying the new fall wardrobes of the women from the insurance company up the street. The phone rang. Still standing in my bay, looking down at Berkeley Street, I answered.

"Mr. Spenser?"

"Yes."

"This is Carol Kenny at the Dowling School. President Garner would like to meet with you, at your earliest convenience."

"How about this morning?" I said.

"Eleven o'clock would be open," she said.

"Okay," I said.

"So today, at eleven, here at the school. Do you need directions?"

I didn't. Pearl and I had been to Dowling so often now that I was pretty sure Pearl wouldn't need directions, either. But Pearl was sick of going. I did some quick phone work with the dog runner to have Pearl cared for all day. I took Pearl and dropped her off, and drove out to Dowling. I parked on the circular drive in front of the school in a space marked ABSOLUTELY NO STUDENT PARKING.

School was in session, and even though the front hall was empty of students, you could feel the repressed energy behind the closed doors of their classrooms. I'd been in prisons that felt this way. Prisons were noisier, and uglier, but they, too, had the same feeling of kinesis restrained that schools did.

I walked to Garner's office and went in. An attractive woman with short salt-and-pepper hair sat at her post outside the great man's office.

"Carol Kenny?" I said.

"Mr. Spenser?"

"Yes."

"Please take a seat," she said. "I'll tell President Garner you're here."

She was wearing a gray suit, a white man-tailored shirt, and sensible black shoes. But when she went to speak to Garner, I noticed that her body deserved better. She was gone for a moment and came back out.

"President Garner will see you shortly," she said.

I smiled politely. Although he had called me, or she had, the way she spoke suggested that I was the supplicant. Make me wait a little. Soften 'em up. Cool.

"May I get you coffee, or a drink of water, or anything?" Carol Kenny said.

"I'll just sit quietly," I said, "and drink in your beauty."

She giggled, which was a little disconcerting. She didn't look like a giggler. I smiled to show I didn't mind a little giggling now and then. And she went back to her computer, her hands moving smoothly over the nearly soundless keys. In a little while, Royce Garner appeared in his doorway and nodded at me.

"You may come in now, Mr. Spenser."

"Hot diggity," I said.

I stood and went past him into his office. Carol Kenny did not look up as I passed. Struggling with her emotions, no doubt. Garner closed the door behind me and indicated a black chair with maple-stained arms in front of his desk. The chair had the school seal on its backrest.

"You may sit there," he said.

I sat. He leaned back in his chair and rested his gaze on me, tapping a pencil softly against the edge of the desk. I bore up as best I could.

"Before I call my attorney," he said after a time, "perhaps you would like to explain to me why you went to my home and upset my wife."

I shook my head.

"Excuse me?" he said.

I shook my head again.

"What does that mean?" he said.

I said, "It means . . ." and shook my head.

"I don't find you amusing," he said.

"Damn," I said.

"Your invasion of my privacy and my wife's is unconscionable. I am prepared to take action against you."

I nodded.

"Goddamn it, say something," Garner said.

"Unconscionable," I said.

Garner was still. He stopped tapping his pencil. He tried glaring at me, but it wasn't very effective.

"Let me say this plainly, sir." Garner was trying to talk with his lips compressed, which is kind of difficult, but he pulled it off. "I will not tolerate any, repeat, any, further harassment. If you come anywhere near my home again, you will hear from my attorneys."

"A fearful prospect," I said. "How about the Rosewood Condominiums in Framingham."

Garner's face remained composed, but his eyes sort of darted.

"What?" he said.

"Where Beth Ann Blair lives," I said. "With a view of the lake?"

Garner shook his head.

"I'm afraid I don't understand," he said.

"You spent the night there last week," I said.

"I'm sorry, you must be mistaken," he said stiffly.

"No. It was you," I said. "How long have you been boffing the good doctor?"

For a moment, something faltered in Garner's gaze, and an ugly thing peeped out. He glanced briefly down at his hands folded in his lap, and when he looked up again, the thing was gone.

"I'm afraid this conversation has concluded," he said.

"Did you know that Beth Ann was also intimate with Jared Clark?" I said.

Garner's eyes darted again. He opened his mouth and closed it, and stood up suddenly. Without a word, he walked around the desk, past my chair, and out through the reception area. I sat for a minute in case he changed his mind. He didn't. After a while, I got up and walked back out through the reception area. Carol Kenny had a startled look frozen on her face, but she tried her best to remain professional. She smiled.

"Meeting over?" she said.

"Yep," I said. "I'm afraid it's finished between us."

She smiled again. "You can find your way out then?"

"I can," I said.

And did.

57

I DIDN'T KNOW WHAT Garner would do next, but I suspected that he'd do it with Beth Ann Blair, and I wanted to be around to see what it was. She wasn't at the Dowling School. From my car, I called her office and hung up when she answered, and drove on over to Channing Hospital and parked and went up to Beth Ann's floor. I went busily into her waiting room. There were two people waiting there, making eye contact with nobody. The door to Beth Ann's office was closed.

I looked around.

"Oops," I said. "Wrong office."

I went out and closed the door. At the end of the corridor, there was a small waiting area with three chairs and a small table on which were the remnants of yesterday's *Wall Street Journal*. I went to the area, sat in one of the chairs, picked up the paper, opened it, and hid behind it. If Garner showed up, I'd spot him. If he called her and she dashed out to meet him, I'd follow her.

People came and went in the corridor, none of them Beth Ann or Garner, none of them paying any attention to me. I read yesterday's market news. Few things are less interesting than yesterday's stock-market results. In a few minutes, a woman and child came out of Beth Ann's and headed for the elevator. An hour later, the two people I'd seen in the waiting room came out. And five minutes later, Beth Ann came out and headed for the elevators, her heels ringing on the floor of the corridor. I hustled down the stairs and out the front door, and was in my car by the time she appeared. There was neither opportunity nor reason for a nondescript rental car. She was paying no attention to anything, and I just needed to keep her in sight, which I did through town and onto the Mass Pike westbound and into a food/fuel service area near Charlton. At the back of the parking lot, near the Dumpster behind the food-court building, with parking spaces open all around it, was a Buick sedan I'd seen before. Beth Ann parked her cute sports car right next to it, on the side away from the Dumpster. I parked a couple of rows back.

Beth Ann got out of her car and walked around the Buick and got in the passenger side. They sat in there together for a while. The door opened on Beth Ann's side and she scrambled out. Garner got out his side. Beth Ann tried to run, and Garner caught her and pushed her against the car. She slapped at him with both hands. He held on to her.

I could hear Beth Ann screaming. I think she was screaming "help," but it was hard to be sure. Garner was trying to
put his hand over her mouth to make her stop screaming. I
think she bit his hand.

I put my car in gear and drove over and parked sideways
behind both their cars and got out. I took hold of Garner
by the back of his coat collar and pulled him away from
Beth Ann.

"You are causing an embarrassing scene," I said.

He twisted and tried to hit me. I slapped his fist away.
Beth Ann tried to run past us. I caught hold of her arm with
my free hand and pulled her back.

"Why can't we all just get along," I said to them.

They both said variations of "Let go of me." He tried to
hit me again. I let go of Beth Ann, and punched him in the
solar plexus. He gasped and bent over and when I let him
go, stumbled back against his car, trying to get his breath.
Beth Ann had started off again. She was wearing three-
inch heels and ran badly in them. I caught her in two steps
and brought her back.

"You have no place to run, anyway," I said.

"He threatened me," she said, her breath heaving. "The
bastard threatened to kill me."

"Did not," Garner gasped.

There was a picnic table on a small patch of grass at the
corner of the parking lot.

"Let us sit over there," I said, "and talk."

"No . . ." Beth Ann said.

Garner had straightened. Still leaning against the car, he
shook his head no.

"I wasn't asking," I said. "Someone has probably called

the cops, and you might want to get calmed down and have a story ready when they get here."

Both of them looked horrified. It was something they'd never considered. The three of us walked across the parking lot and sat at the table. In the distance, I could hear a siren.

"You had a little sort of lovers' spat," I said. "I, in a friendly way, intervened, and now we've talked it out and no one has any complaints to register."

Both of them heard the siren, too. Neither of them said anything. Beth Ann was still flushed, but Garner was very pale.

58

A STATE POLICE CAR pulled up in front of the restaurant building, and a big trooper got out and went in. In a moment, he came back out with two people. They talked. He nodded. They pointed toward us. He nodded. As he walked across the lot toward the picnic table, a second cruiser pulled in and parked behind his.

The big trooper stopped at our table. I recognized him. It was one of the two Staties who, at DiBella's request, had brought Animal to the state maintenance shed for me to reason with. He looked at me. I looked at him.

"DiBella's friend," the cop said.

"Sort of," I said.

"I understand there was some trouble here," the cop said, and looked at Garner and Beth Ann.

Garner gathered himself.

"I'm afraid it was just a lovers' spat, Officer."

The cop looked at Beth Ann. "You agree with that?" he said.

She smiled at him, which was pretty impressive.

"Yes. I feel like a fool," she said. "But Roy and I . . . we lost our tempers at the same time."

"You?" the cop said to me.

"I happened upon them, and intervened and managed to reconcile them."

The cop looked at me and shook his head. But he didn't comment.

"Either of you wish to file any kind of complaint?" he said to the happy couple.

"No, sir," Garner said.

"We're fine," Beth Ann said.

The trooper looked at me. "Everything's fine," I said.

"You people better learn to settle your differences another way," he said. "I get another complaint and I won't be so easy about it."

He and I both knew that was a crock. He hadn't even taken their names. But he and I both knew also that idle threats work sometimes.

"It won't happen again, Officer," Garner said.

"Absolutely not," Beth Ann said and smiled again at the cop.

The smile was effective. It managed to suggest somehow that she'd like to have sex with him. Which, of course, could have been true. The cop looked at me again.

"That your Mustang there?" he said.

"I'll move it at once," I said.

He nodded. "You all have a nice day," he said.

He walked back across the parking lot and stopped next to the second cruiser. He spoke to the second cop for a few minutes, then got into his own car and both of them pulled away. The three of us at our picnic table were silent for a bit.

Then Beth Ann looked at Garner and said, "You cock-sucker."

"You keep your damned mouth shut," he said to her. "Just remember what I told you, and keep your damn mouth shut."

Garner stood then and stalked away toward his car, which he couldn't drive away in because I had him blocked.

"Could you move your damned car?" he said.

59

Before I moved my car, I reached in and took the keys out of Beth's. When Garner was gone, I walked back to the picnic table, sat across from her, and put the keys on the table.

She didn't speak. Neither did I. We listened to the steady sound of traffic from the pike. A burly woman in pink shorts and a white T-shirt walked a very small fuzzy white dog near us. I smiled at the dog. The dog paid me no attention.

"What do you see in him?" I said after a while.

Beth Ann looked at the table and shook her head.

"He's kind of soft and dumpy," I said. "But he's very annoying."

Beth Ann shook her head again. It might have been disagreement. It might have been regret. The white dog accomplished its mission on the small plot of grass, and the burly woman took it away. She was wearing some sort of sandals with elevated soles, and she walked with a lumbering wobble. From my inside coat pocket I took a copy of the photograph I'd found in Beth Ann's freezer and placed it on the table in front of her, next to her keys. She looked down at it without any reaction for a moment. Then she said, "It was you," and turned the photo facedown on the table, and put her face into her hands and moaned. I didn't say anything. No one was near us. I sat, quietly listening to the traffic and the wind and the occasional scraps of conversation that the wind brought us from people as they walked to their cars. The cooking smell from the restaurant was strong.

"You have it too," she said finally.

"Too?" I said.

"He has a copy."

"Garner?"

"Yes."

I sat back. It wasn't that I couldn't think of questions. I thought of too many, and they were all jockeying for position.

With her face still pressed into her hands, Beth Ann said, "It's not what you think."

"I think it's a picture of you naked with Jared Clark when he was even younger than he is now."

She kept her face in her hands and shook her head again.

"Oh, God," she said.

While she was contemplating whatever ruins she saw in the palms of her hands, I got my questions sequenced.

"Garner has a copy of this picture?"

Face in hands, she nodded.

"How did he get it?"

"He . . . he's so weird," she said. "At night, sometimes he goes through the school, searching lockers."

"What lockers," I said.

"Student lockers, faculty lockers. I don't know why. He said he was making sure there were no drugs or guns or anything."

"You believe that."

She shook her head.

"What do you believe?" I said.

No hurry, plenty of time, ask all the questions, keep the strands straight, one strand at a time.

"He's sick."

"And it excites him to prowl?"

She nodded.

"Did he find this picture in your locker or Jared's?" I said.

"Jared's."

"And what use has he put it to?" I said.

She kept her face in her hands.

"What use?"

"Is that what you see in him?"

"He's a disgusting little prick," she said.

I nodded.

"He makes me . . ." She shook her head.

"If you have sex with him," I said, "he won't tell."

She inhaled audibly. I waited. She exhaled even more audibly, as if she'd been running.

"Yes," she said.

"How long has this been going on?"

"Two years."

"Which makes the photograph more than two years old," I said.

"Yes."

"So Jared was how old when it was taken."

She was silent.

"Fifteen?" I said.

She shook her head.

"How old?" I said.

"Fourteen."

"So tell me about that," I said.

She was silent again, framing her thoughts, no doubt.

"Take your time," I said.

She did. But finally, she raised her face and looked at me. Her eyes were red, but she wasn't crying. The bright sunlight penetrated her makeup, and underneath it she looked haggard and older than she was.

"It's not what you think," she said.

"It rarely is," I said.

"Do you believe in love, Mr. Spenser?"

"I do."

She had full eye contact with me, and she leaned a little toward me when she spoke.

"Jared and I love each other," she said.

"How nice," I said.

"Do you find that so hard to believe that someone like me would love a boy such as he?"

"I do," I said.

She smiled sadly. She was regrouping swiftly.

"I do too," she said. "And yet . ... and yet it's true."

"Are you aware that he is retarded?" I said.

"He absolutely is not," she said. "You think I wouldn't know?"

"Yes," I said. "I think you wouldn't know."

"He's reticent perhaps, a kind of dreamy poetic reticence."

"The best kind," I said.

"It began," Beth Ann said, "when he was sent to me by one of his teachers. They felt he was withdrawn. He was so quiet in class."

"To what did you attribute that?"

"Do you understand psychology, Mr. Spenser?"

"I've been in love for a long time with one of the great shrinks in America," I said. "I've absorbed a little."

"So you do believe in love."

"Yes."

"There's a medical condition," Beth Ann said, "called failure to flourish. Have you heard of that?"

"Yes."

"Jared has the emotional and psychological equivalent of that disease," she said.

"Caused by?" I said.

"A lack of mattering. A lack of centrality. No one thought he was important. He lacked self-esteem. He wasn't loved sufficiently."

I had been listening with my hands pressed together and my fingertips against my chin. I pointed at her with my pressed hands.

"And you had a cure," I said.

"You . . . however you make it sound," Beth Ann said. "Yes. I felt that if I could love him enough, I could bring him to a fully realized life."

"Worked out good so far," I said.

It was as if she hadn't heard me. And maybe she hadn't. She seemed deeply engaged in spinning her web.

"And in the process," she said, "I came to love him, as I know he loved me."

I nodded. "Who took the picture?" I said.

"Jared. He had one of those new digital cameras."

"The kind you hook up to a computer?" I said.

"Yes. It had a timer attachment."

"Did you have sex?"

"Then, when the picture was taken?"

"Then," I said, "later. Anytime. Were you having sex with Jared."

"We made love," Beth Ann said with great dignity.

"Did you get to spend time together aside from making love?" I said.

"It was difficult, as you might imagine. The prejudices of the middle class are fearful, as you may know. We took our time, and our passion, when we could."

"And you saw no hint of functional retardation?" I said.

"No. Of course not. His grades were good. He may have seemed slow to some because he talked slowly. But he talked slowly because he thought so deeply."

"As so many fourteen-year-olds do," I said.

"He is unusual far beyond his chronological age," Beth Ann said.

"Good point," I said. "Most kids his age are not in jail for murder."

"You can believe what you wish," she said, and sat back so that her breasts pushed against her sweater.

Whoops.

"Unless your degrees are fraudulent," I said, "you would be in a position better than mine to understand how unlikely it is that a woman like you would fall in love with a boy like Jared."

She pointed her breasts at me. Both barrels.

"You think it's impossible?" she said.

"Few things are impossible," I said. "I think it is improbable."

"So what would be your explanation?"

"I'd guess some sort of psychosexual pathology on your part," I said.

"That's disgusting."

"So what happened?" I said.

"Happened?"

"To the relationship."

"Garner made me break it off," she said.

"He refused to share?"

"That, too, is disgusting," she said.

"But true?"

"Yes. He said I had to stop seeing Jared or he'd destroy me professionally."

"With the picture," I said.

"Yes."

"Did you tell Jared?"

"I tried to be as kind as I could be," she said. "I told him the school knew of our relationship, and we would have to stop seeing each other for a while."

"How'd he take it?"

"How do you think he would take it. He was devastated."

"Do you suppose that made him go off on the school?"

"I don't know what to think," she said.

"You didn't rush to his rescue when he did go off," I said.

"What could I do?"

"You might have shared what you knew."

"How could I help him by destroying myself?" she said.

Her whole bearing had intensified, as if she had been re-hydrated. I had a private bet with myself where we were going.

"You might have avoided describing him to me in terms of a classic school shooter. Isolated. Bullied unmercifully. That kind of thing."

"He'd already confessed and been arrested," she said. She was starting to breathe more heavily, and her breasts moved as if rebelling against the sweater. "I didn't see what good it would do to call attention to myself."

"You know anything about Wendell Grant?" I said.

"Nothing," she said. "I don't believe I ever spoke with him."

I picked the photograph up off the table and put it back in my inside pocket.

"What are you going to do?" she said.

"I don't know," I said.

"Do you suppose you could make Royce give me back my picture?"

"Probably," I said.

"Would you give me back your copy?"

"No."

"It's all I have of Jared," she said.

"You've probably had too much of Jared already," I said.

Her eyes widened and her voice softened. I could hear her breathing.

"I need your help," she said.

"You do," I said.

"Can't you help me," she said.

"Probably not," I said

"I don't like my arrangement with Royce," she said. "But I do it because he makes me."

"Uh-huh."

"I want to escape from him," she said.

"Uh-huh."

"I would like an arrangement with you," she said.

"I need time to work on my poetic depth," I said and stood up. "I'll get back to you."

60

"So she was fucking this guy to keep him from telling everyone that she was fucking this kid?" Cleary said.

"Well put," I said.

"And the kid was underage when she was fucking him?"

"Almost certainly," I said.

"And you can prove this?"

"Whoops," I said.

"You can't prove it," Cleary said.

"I can probably prove it. I got the naked photo."

"Evidence of a possible felony," Cleary said. "I'll have to examine it closely."

"Yeah," I said. "Take a number. DiBella's already got first dibs."

Cleary smiled.

"The photo's pretty good leverage."

"With her," I said. "I have only her word with Garner."

"But you know they were spending the night together."

"Yes."

"So why do you want to talk with the kid again?" Cleary said.

"I need to know where the love affair with Beth Ann fits in to what he did."

"And I should help you with this?"

"In the interest of justice?" I said.

"Justice?" Cleary said. "This office wants convictions, not justice."

"You'll convict him," I said. "But maybe the circumstances would mitigate the sentence."

"His sentence gets mitigated and the fucking community will be in open rebellion," Cleary said.

"Lot of heavy stuff happened to that kid," I said.

"A lot of heavy stuff happened to other kids, in the school, when he killed them," Cleary said.

"I need to know what happened," I said.

"Spenser, get away from me," Cleary said. "His lawyer's already conceded. Nobody wants the sentence mitigated. His parents even want him long gone."

"I might be able to do something about the lawyer," I said.

"Well, wouldn't that work out good for me?" Cleary said. "If I am really cooperative, I can turn this case into a major headache for myself."

"The woman may have caused this," I said.

"Even if she did," Cleary said, "even if he had a better lawyer, he's going away."

"We need to know," I said.

"They don't want a better lawyer. They want him gone."

"Maybe I could persuade them," I said.

"You got another lawyer in mind?"

"Rita Fiore," I said.

"The best defense attorney in the fucking state," Cleary said. "And you want me to help you bring her on board?"

"Exactly," I said.

Cleary looked at me. I looked back.

"You're going to get your conviction," I said. "Might as well have some justice on the side."

Cleary kept looking at me. I smiled at him warmly.

Finally, he said, "Jesus Christ!" and leaned forward and picked up the phone.

61

"I DON'T WANT to talk to you," Jared Clark said when they brought him in and sat him down.

"I know," I said. "Nobody does."

"Well," he said. "I won't."

"Beth Ann Blair says that she was in love with you," I said. His eyes widened. "What?" he said.

"Beth Ann Blair says she is in love with you and that you are in love with her."

He laughed. I didn't know why, and I suspect he didn't know why. But there it was: ha, ha.

"We're not supposed to tell anybody," he said.

"She told," I said.

"She told you she loves me."

"Yes," I said.

He laughed the same odd and inappropriate laugh.

"You want to tell me about that?" I said.

"She already told you."

"She told me how she feels," I said. "I was wondering how you feel."

"She really told you," he said.

"Yes."

"Honest to God?"

"Honest to God," I said. "You love her?"

He laughed. It wasn't a laugh about funny. I winked at him.

"Even if you didn't," I said, "Pretty good in bed, huh?"

His face got red. "Don't say that."

"Sorry," I said.

"I love her. She loves me. When people love each other, that's what they do."

"Go to bed," I said.

He nodded firmly.

"When did you start to love each other?" I said.

"Since ninth grade."

"Wow," I said.

"Where does Mr. Garner fit in."

"Fuck him," Jared said.

"He knew you and Beth Ann were in love," I said.

"He was going to not let us," Jared said.

All of a sudden I saw it, all of it, full-formed, as if a magic lantern threw the patterns on a screen.

"You had to stop him," I said.

"Yes."

"She wanted you to," I said.

"Yes."

"But you didn't know for sure how to stop him, so you went to Dell, and he helped you."

Jared nodded.

"But when you went to do it, Garner wasn't there."

He nodded.

"And things got out of hand," I said.

"Dell kept shooting," Jared said softly.

"And you never said why you did it, because it would hurt Beth Ann."

There were tears now. I didn't blame him. I felt like crying, too.

"So you got the chance to be a stand-up guy," I said.

He nodded. He was crying audibly. The tears were rolling down his face.

"You were going to shoot Garner."

Nod.

"And Dell was going to cover you."

Nod.

"Dell plan this out mostly?"

"Yes. He knew about things like that. From Animal."

"You didn't plan on getting caught."

He shook his head.

"Dell had a different plan," I said.

Jared looked at me blankly.

"You shoot anyone?"

"No."

I could hear myself breathing. I needed more oxygen than I was getting. My throat needed to loosen. My stomach needed to unclench.

"We was going to get married," Jared said, "when I was eighteen."

"Next year," I said.

He nodded. "You think she still loves me?" he said.

I took in some more air.

"Absolutely," I said. "She loves you, and adores you, and admires very much how brave you are."

He nodded his head and continued to nod it while he sat there and cried.

62

RITA WAS WEARING a black pantsuit today, with a green silk T-shirt. She walked to her big picture window and studied her view of the south shore. Her pantsuit fit her very well. We were high, and there was no city sound, and her office was big and had a thick carpet, and there was almost no office noise.

"Okay," she said with her back to me, which was not a bad thing. "You say that since he was in the ninth grade . . . how old is that?"

"Fourteen, fifteen," I said. "I believe he was fourteen when it began."

"Since he was fourteen, he's been having sex with the school shrink who is, what, thirty-five? Forty?"

"Somewhere in there," I said.

"And the kid is functionally retarded."

"Mildly," I said.

"And the school president . . . what kind of high school has a president?"

"It's a private high school," I said, "and it's aiming to become a junior college as well."

"And the president finds out and blackmails the shrink into having sex with him, and she is feeling, ah, violated?"

"Violated is good," I said.

"She talks the kid into killing the president," Rita said. "Thus freeing her from his unwanted attentions and allowing the two lovebirds, Jared and Beth Ann, to be together again."

"Until Jared turns eighteen and they can marry," I said.

"Gee, I didn't know he was the marrying kind. . . ." Rita said. "Makes him more interesting."

"He may be a little gun-shy right now," I said.

She turned away from the window and looked at me. Her suit fit very well in the front, too.

"Aren't they all," she said. "So, he connects with the school badass, who hooks them up with a gangbanger, who gets them guns and teaches them how to shoot, and they go into the school like two commandos, only the president isn't there that day, perhaps out tapping the school shrink against her wishes? So the kids start shooting the place up, except that our kid, Jared, says he didn't shoot. Any way to prove that?"

"Probably not."

"And the school badass says he did?"

"Wendell Grant, yes."

"You don't suppose the cops told him that if he ratted out his pal, he'd get a break?"

"Cops do that?" I said.

"He's not going to get a break," Rita said. "Not for shooting up a school. He'd lose nothing by saying Jared didn't shoot."

"He might just enjoy taking Jared down with him," I said.

"Not easy," she said.

Her mouth was open. She was tapping her bottom teeth with a ballpoint pen. Her thick, red hair came to her shoulders. She was something to see.

"You have a functionally retarded underaged boy whose parents really want to get rid of him," I said. "Who was sexually exploited by an older woman. You oughtta be able to do something with that."

"Jared's going away somewhere," Rita said.

"And probably should," I said. "But maybe he shouldn't spend the rest of his life somewhere, and maybe it should be a kinder somewhere."

"If such a place exists," Rita said. "Will Beth Ann Blair stick to her story?"

"I don't know," I said.

"And Jared?"

"I don't know," I said.

"I love a nice, solid case," Rita said.

I shrugged.

"The kid deserves better than he's getting," I said.

She looked at me and smiled, which was something to see in itself, and walked to her desk and sat in her big leather partner's chair and put her feet up and tapped her teeth some more.

"Tell me something," Rita said. "You have stuck by this kid, whom you barely know, like he was your own. But you don't seem interested at all in the other one."

"Grant?"

"Yes. Don't you suppose he might have serious problems that weren't addressed? Doesn't he need help? Isn't he a kid, too? Should he spend the rest of his life in jail?"

"Nobody hired me to stick with Grant," I said.

"That's it?" Rita said.

"Yes."

"That's all?" Rita said.

"That's all there is," I said.

"No right or wrong, nothing like that?"

"Right or wrong?" I said. "Rita, you're a lawyer."

"I know, never tell that I said that."

We were quiet for a moment.

"There's thousands of people need saving," I said. "I can't save them all. Hell, I can't save half the ones I try to save."

"So you let chance decide?" Rita said. "Someone hires you?"

"Chance and choice," I said. "I don't take every case."

"How do you decide?" Rita said.

"I'm not sure," I said. "I usually know it when I see it."

"You can't save everybody," Rita said.

"And if I try, I end up saving nobody," I said.

"And saving one is better than saving none," Rita said.

I nodded. Rita looked at me silently before she spoke.

"Do you know what I bill an hour?" she said.

"I believe I do."

"How you going to pay me?"

"I'll give you every cent I earn on this case from here on," I said.

She looked at me some more and smiled wider.

"They fired you," she said. "Didn't they?"

"Well," I said. "Yuh."

"And you're offering me half of that."

"Yuh."

Rita laughed softly and flipped the ballpoint pen onto her desk.

"I'll take it," she said.

63

I WAS IN MY OFFICE. Pearl was asleep on the couch. It was raining outside, and the colorful umbrellas over boots and fashionable raincoats were flowering once more on Berkeley Street. The office door opened. Pearl's head went up. Royce Garner came in and closed the door behind him and pointed a gun at me.

"I'm going to kill you," he said.

With his orotund voice, he sounded like Richard Nixon. Pearl growled.

He turned toward her with the gun, and I shot him at an angle in the backside, so that the bullet passed through and lodged in the far wall. Confined by the small room, the gunshot hurt my ears. Garner fell over. Pearl jumped from the couch and scuttled behind my desk. Still holding the gun, I patted her as I went past her to Garner.

"Should have kept the gun on me," I said. "I'm a lot more dangerous than Pearl."

"You shot me," he gasped. "You shot me."

I picked up his gun carefully and went back to my desk and put it in a large plastic Baggie. I put my gun back in the holster. Then I called 911 and ordered up an ambulance.

"Help me," he said. "I'll die if you don't help me."

"No you won't," I said. "You got shot in the ass. You're not even bleeding that bad."

I went to the sink and got a hand towel and folded it up tightly and walked to Garner and squatted down beside him.

"Oh, God," he said. "This hurts. I'm bleeding."

I pressed the towel against his wound.

"Roll over so you're lying on the towel," I said. "It'll be like a pressure bandage."

"I can't move," he said.

"Oh," I said. "Well, maybe you will bleed to death."

He groaned and struggled over onto his side and groaned again, but his weight was on the wound and the towel. I stood and leaned my butt against the front edge of my desk. Pearl peered bravely around the edge of the desk at Garner.

"Ow," he said. "It's, like, burning."

"Ambulance is coming," I said.

"I wasn't . . . going to . . . shoot you," Garner said. "I just wanted to talk."

"Which is why you brought a gun and pointed it at me and said . . ." I dropped my voice, imitating him: "I'm going to kill you."

"I wasn't going . . . to."

"Sure you were," I said. "I'm the only one that knew about the pictures and all. With me dead, you'd have everything back under control. You would be president of a nice junior college. The kid would be away for life. Beth Ann would be hauling your ashes again, and you'd have a nice alternative to the alcoholic oinker you married."

"No," Garner said. "No, I was just going to talk. I can give you some money, maybe. I'm an educator. We don't have a lot."

I shook my head. "Pal, you don't have anything at all," I said.

I could hear the siren sound in the distance. Pearl crept out from behind the desk and went to Garner and sniffed at him. She was interested in the blood.

"Don't let her hurt me," he said.

I said, "Pearl."

And she came.

I said, "Sit."

And she sat.

I knew it wouldn't last, but it was pretty impressive.

Two uniforms came into my office first, then two EMTs, then Belson. When Pearl saw Belson, she stood and wagged her tail and walked over to him. The EMTs got busy with Garner.

"I saw the call and recognized the address," Belson said. "I didn't want to miss out on anything."

"Too bad it's not a happier occasion," I said.

I went to my desk and got Garner's gun and handed it in its bag to Belson. He took it and handed it on to one of the uniforms.

"This might be evidence," Belson said. "Try not to lose it."

"He tried to kill me, officer," Garner said as importantly as he could. The EMTs had pulled his pants down to put a pressure bandage on the wound, so that sounding important wasn't easy. Belson looked down at him for a moment or two, scratching Pearl's ear absently.

"Goddamn," he said to me. "You got another one."

64

THE MEETING was in the big, flossy conference room next to Rita's office on the thirty-ninth floor at Cone, Oakes, which was much too big for our small group. Finger sandwiches were served, and fresh fruit, and coffee, and bottled water. The coffee and the water were about the same temperature. Cleary was there; and Richard Leeland, theoretically representing Jared Clark; and Alex Taglio, Grant's lawyer; and me. The Clarks had declined Rita's invitation, as had Wendell Grant's mother. Probably heard about the coffee.

"I've taken the liberty of providing each of you with an outline of the situation in which we find ourselves," Rita said, "which could be described as a mess."

"Can't tell the players without a scorecard," Alex Taglio said.

"Correct," Rita said, and went through the case, point by point, to where we were now. She was in full-power costume today. Black suit, white shirt, expensive pearls. She looked beautiful and flashy and formidable.

Which she was.

"We have some administrative matters to get out of the way," she said when she had finished her summary.

She turned to Leeland and gave him a promising smile. Rita was never unaware of the amount of heat she generated.

"Mr. Cleary and I have talked," she said. "And we both feel it best if you resign the case and I take over as Jared Clark's attorney."

"Excuse me?" Leeland said.

"I'm a far better lawyer than you are, Mr. Leeland," Rita said. "And your client will be much better off."

Rita deferred to Cleary.

"Mr. Cleary?" she said.

"Richard," Cleary said. "I don't know why you'd want to stay with this thing, but if you do, and you insist, I've already talked with Judge Costello about having you replaced."

Leeland stared at him. "By her?" he said.

"Yes."

Leeland opened his mouth and closed it. He looked around the room. Nobody else said anything.

"On what basis?" he said.

"What was your last criminal case?" Cleary said.

"I . . ." Leeland said. He waved his hand aimlessly and shook his head.

"Exactly," Cleary said. "You are not, by training or experience, competent to represent someone in a case of this nature. You tried to help out the family, like a good friend, but now, as we are beginning to push and shove, it's time to let you off the hook."

Leeland looked around the room. No one interceded on his behalf. He picked up the handout that Rita had given him and folded it and put it in his briefcase. He stood up.

"I guess there's no reason for me to stay," he said.

"I'll take that as your resignation speech," Cleary said.

"Yeah," Leeland said. "Sure."

He walked out of the conference room and closed the door behind him.

"Turning to the next matter," Rita said, "I understand that both Mr. Spenser and Dr. Dix, as a condition of the interview with Jared Clark, reached an agreement with Mr. Cleary that Dr. Dix's findings not be used in court."

Cleary took a drink of his coffee and frowned and looked at it for a moment and put the cup back in the saucer.

"The situation has changed," Cleary said. "I am willing to waive that agreement."

A secretary came softly into the conference room and said something to Rita.

"Alex," Rita said. "Phone call. You can take it in my office."

"You tell them I was in a meeting?" Taglio said.

"It's your office, sir," the secretary said. "They insisted."

"No cell phone?" Rita said.

"I shut it off," Taglio said and got up and went out.

"Now that we are mostly on the same page," Rita said, "do we have a plan?"

"The case has to go to court," Cleary said. "We don't try

these kids and convict them of something, Bethel County will go crazy."

Rita nodded.

"I understand that," she said.

"And," Cleary said, "even if that were not a consideration, I believe these kids should be tried, convicted, and punished for what they did."

"No big argument here," Rita said.

"I believe the system works," Cleary said, "when the playing field is level. I plan to prosecute vigorously, expect you to defend vigorously, and see what happens. Thanks to you, pal," Cleary nodded toward me, "things have leveled up."

"He is industrious," Rita said. "How about Beth Ann Blair and Royce Garner."

"We should be able to come up with some suitable charges against them, plus what Boston does on the assault charge. I'll prosecute them vigorously when I'm through prosecuting the kids vigorously."

"If you bring the charges before we try the kids," Rita said, "it'll give us some leverage to ensure their full cooperation."

"As long as we all remember that this is not a cooperative venture."

"I know," Rita said. "It's an adversarial procedure. But, at least in theory, our goal is the same."

"Justice?" Cleary said.

Rita shrugged. Taglio came back into the room and sat down.

"We were going to talk about severance?" he said.

"I was going to get there," Rita said.

Taglio shook his head. "Somebody shanked Wendell Grant."

"Dead?" Cleary said.

"Yep."

"He was supposed to be kept separate," Cleary said.

"I know," Taglio said.

Rita looked down at the yellow pad on the table in front of her and crossed off an item.

65

PEARL WAS ASLEEP on the living-room couch. I was having the first drink of the day, sitting at my kitchen counter, watching the ball game and trying to keep myself under control. It was September. The Sox were still in it, and this might be the year again . . . or not.

Suddenly, Pearl sat bolt upright on the couch, her ears forward, and stared at my front door unwaveringly. There was the sound of a key in the lock. Pearl began to whimper softly. I did not, being more restrained. The door opened, and Susan came in with a shoulder bag. Pearl bolted over the back of the couch and rushed at her. Susan put her shoulder bag on the floor and crouched down. Pearl capered over and around her, lapping her face and making small crying sounds. I felt the same way, but there was no room for both of us in my small hallway. Instead, in an act of great symbolic import, I picked up the remote and shut off the Sox game.

Susan stood and worked her way around Pearl and came to the counter. I got off the stool and put my arms out, and there she was. I was complete again. Pearl weaseled around us as we hugged.

"The limo took me home," Susan said. "And I unpacked and took a bath and changed my clothes and came right over."

The room seemed full of oxygen.

"Why the hurry?" I said.

My voice sounded odd to me, and remote.

"Because I have missed you so badly I couldn't breathe," Susan said. "And I love you so much I could explode."

"Wow," I said.

"Exactly," she said.

Pearl didn't like being shut out of the bedroom, but she had grown somewhat used to it, and didn't yowl. When it was appropriate, Susan got up, a little uneasy, as always, about being naked while upright, and opened the bedroom door. Pearl joined us.

"Home," Susan said with me on one side of her and Pearl on the other.

"Wherever we are," I said.

"Yes."

We talked for a long time. She about the conference at Duke, me about the Jared Clark situation. Pearl lost interest and fell asleep with her head on Susan's thigh, which made it impossible for Susan to get under the covers without disturbing Pearl, which I knew she wouldn't do. I did not lose interest. I could listen to Susan talking to me, or me talking to Susan, for as long as either of us could sustain it. And when neither of us could, our silences together were just as symphonic.

"Jared really didn't have much of a chance," Susan said.

"No."

I had my arm around Susan's shoulders. Her head was on my chest.

"The other kid probably didn't, either," Susan said.

"No."

"Lot of kids don't have a chance, do they," Susan said.

"You and I see the adult residue of that every day," I said.

"Perhaps the one absolute essential to growing up well is being tough enough," Susan said.

"Like us," I said.

"Just like us," Susan said. "But maybe not so lucky."

"I'd have found you," I said, "with or without luck."

Susan smiled and kissed me gently on the mouth.

"Probably not," she said. "But if someone could, it would be you."

Pearl shifted her position, and Susan whipped the covers over herself. I smiled.

"At last," I said.

"I wonder why I'm so uneasy naked," she said.

"Maybe it's the gimlet-eyed lechery of my gaze," I said.

"Probably," she said.

We lay quietly, listening to our silence for a while.

"What will happen to him?" Susan said.

"He'll do time," I said. "He's confessed. We know he

was in that school with a loaded gun. He's the only one who really knows if he shot somebody."

"But . . . ?"

"But aside from being hotter than the rockets' red glare," I said, "Rita Fiore is a goddamned genius."

"So he has some hope," Susan said.

"The answer to that is more your department," I said. "His parents have put him aside. The love of his life is a child molester. He's going to be convicted in one way or another of a capital crime. How much hope is he likely to have?"

"Some hope is better than no hope," Susan said.

"They teach you that at Harvard?" I said.

"No," Susan said. "I learned that from you."

Robert B. Parker is the author of more than fifty books, including the bestsellers *Bad Business* and *Melancholy Baby*. He lives in Boston.